Adam's First Wife

Sarah
my RHS Queen
Enjoy the journey
buckets of time
+ possibility
Love
Darlene

ADAM'S FIRST WIFE

The Saga of Lilith

DARLENE DAUPHIN

ISBN: 9781796902563
Copyright 2019

Front Cover illustration by TD Dauphin

PROLOGUE

ON THE STEEP and craggy bluff overlooking the place where the great rivers join, two people stand in shadowed profile against the tempered fire of the sunrise. The tall man uses one hand to hold his staff. The other arm rests around the shoulders of an adolescent girl. She looks in the direction that he points. Her chin is held defiantly up and forward to face the world toward which her father gestures. It is unusual to see a father and daughter in such a stance because generally, fathers reveal the world to their sons. But here, in this place, this man knows already that his daughter belongs to the world beyond this kingdom surrounded by water.

In this lush patch of land, life flourished at the dawn of time. People of the river kingdom enjoyed the luxury of an abundance of the ingredients necessary for their well-being. Fertile soil in this place allowed these people to produce the best array of crops far and wide, while many other fruits and grains grew naturally. Men of the tribe cast their nets, trolling the rivers' depths for the wide variety of marine life abounding in those waters. All about the grassy plains of the foothills to the east, hunters of the tribe made quick work of slaying enough game to feed the people. Because nothing was wasted in this society, the majority of any animal carcass was used productively. Hides were tanned, dyed and worked to a variety of finishes. Some of the very supple skins were cut and dyed for use as clothing. Especially useful during the cold season, this clothing was both durable and comfortable. Craftsmen finished other hides into a multitude of useful and beautiful leather products. Ivory from the teeth and tusks of animals was fashioned into both jewelry and tools by local artisans. The intricate carving and trace work of these carvers was renowned throughout the region. Exquisite combs carved from ivory were used from generation to generation. Fibers obtained from the crops were woven into cloth of several types. Traders prized the cloth products of these people because of the unique dyes and patterns used in their making. The river people were a self-sufficient civilization whose needs were met within the unique area of land that they inhabited. They enjoyed trading relationships with varied foreign peoples who valued their goods and products. Peaceful and skilled in the arts necessary to create a comfortable life, no other people were as fortunate. Indeed it was said that the gods smiled upon them, they lived in paradise.

1

THE DAY OF her marriage ceremony dawned with a bright, sweet quietness that befitted the solemnity of the occasion. She lay quietly on the intricately woven mat, refusing to open her eyes. Once she did open her eyes, Lilith knew, her life would change forever. Today, she was to wed the young man whom she loved, who was her heart's desire. Her prayer to the gods was that it was not all a dream, that she had not imagined this whole last period of the moon, the time of her betrothal. If it was all something that she had imagined, when she opened her eyes and discovered that it was not the day she had dreamed of, she might die. Taking a deep breath, the girl slowly opened first one eye and then the other. In the straw basket next to her mat, the exquisite garment lay folded. "Ahhhh," she thought. "It is truly so." By the gods, she had thought that this day would never happen because her beloved Adaama had been a most reluctant suitor.

Unlike most others, her betrothal did not happen easily, nor did it occur immediately following the day of the ceremony celebrating her introduction to womanhood. Though she was undoubtedly the young woman who inspired the most conversation on the day and who attracted the largest number of suitors, Lilith was decidedly unhappy with its outcome. By the end of the feast day, all of the girls had been presented and the eager suitors had presented gifts, made their intentions known. It had been a glorious day of festivities for the village. Children darted in and out among the adults, enjoying the chance to meet others from neighboring areas. The atmosphere was charged with excited merriment. During the feast that followed, the villagers were buzzing with the news of the day. Despite the many interested parties who pressed suit upon her father, Lilith's insides churned with dread. As she had suspected, Adaama had not expressed his interest, nor had he even attended the ceremony. Because more than a dozen suitors presented offers to her family, there needed to be a reasonable time for consideration of all interested parties. Her only hope was that something would change soon.

Early the next morning Lilith and her best friend, the prettily petite Naiimi, rushed to meet at the laundry site on the river. Older women of the tribe glanced admiringly at the pair. Never had they seen such conscientious young women. On the day before, these two girls had participated in the ceremony that designated womanhood and they could soon be chosen as brides. Few times in their lives did the river women enjoy the luxury of ignoring chores. For these two, this morning could have been excused. However, the friends desired to discuss the previous day's events and moved slightly apart from the group.

"Where was he, Naiimi?" Lilith spoke quietly.

"No one seems to know. Bhutu also spoke of his absence." Her friend went through the motions of pounding the soiled clothes. Bhutu was her betrothed and Adaama's constant male companion throughout the period of growing up.

"He seemed more concerned that his friend was not present, than that my father was announcing our betrothal at the feast."

"Silly girl, you know that this is not true. Bhutu was so very happy. I overheard him telling my brother of his relief that the day had finally arrived. After all, you have been promised since we were at our mothers' feet." Lilith forgot some of her own discontent when considering her petite friend's good fortune. Bhutu was of small stature, but still well built and pleasing to look upon. His charm lay in his fluid tongue. He had the ability to make light of every situation and was always the one to keep the group laughing.

"You are always so wise, but just a little of me wishes that some surprises awaited me. However, Bhutu is a dear boy and I should consider myself very lucky." For a moment she thanked her blessed stars. Bhutu and Naaimi, had long been promised. They had grown up understanding that their lives were destined to intertwine and looked forward to their marriage. The depth of their friendship appeared to make a wonderful foundation for the coming union. In her typically cheery way, her mind shifted back to the previous day's events.

"Poor Edekke, Did you see that person speaking to her father at length? He is seeking a third wife, who will be little more than a handmaid to his horrible First Wife." Naiimi's tinkling laughter rang out in the morning air.

Lilith made a face, "Oh yes. She is such a sweet natured girl. It would be a difficult life. Ugh, the thought of bedding such a man. Did you see that he looks very much like those large birds with the very long legs?"

"We should not speak of such things, Lilith." Naiimi's eyes were quickly cast down as the conversation dissolved into nervous laughter.

A chorus of giggles followed as they discussed each of the other girls, their suitors and village gossip in general. When both the task and conversation were complete, the sun had found its way high overhead and the two girls set foot to the path back to the village.

It was time for the midday meal, which was generally communal. Others were making their way from the river, forest and grasslands. In the distance a lone figure became visible. As he neared, the girls saw that it was Adaama, returning from the hilly grasslands with the obvious bounty from a hunting trip strung across his shoulders. Men of the village usually hunted in groups, never less than pairs. Most stopped to behold the sight, as it was strange to all that saw him returning. They lived in a dangerous time, but the people of the river took care to protect one another. Such an unsanctioned solo foray into the grasslands would surely cause him to be scolded by the elders. As he came closer, he appeared to be without concern. From the expression on his face it did not appear that he either anticipated, or cared about, any negative response. Bhutu and another of the young men rushed to greet him. They were admiring and examining the dead animals when the headman approached the group. Even from the distance his displeasure was obvious. Adaama's expression was much less comfortable when he finally reached the eating area after storing the fresh game. He avoided eye contact with Lilith and Naiimi though he was only a few feet away.

Lilith could not help but look at him and admire his appearance. Adaama was unique when compared to the other young men. Standing a few hands taller than Lilith, his broad shoulders and sturdy legs were majestically formed, but his skin was colored like the morning sky at dawn, a pale pinkish golden shade. His hair was of the same brilliant shade as the morning sun.

Others like him were born from time to time, but he was the first in this village to survive past childhood. Since it was difficult to shield them from the ravages of the sun, those children seldom left the huts of their families. While they were rare, it seemed that some families, more than others, produced these golden children. It was said that in Adaama's family several had survived. His grandmother, who lived in a neighboring village, was almost as pale as he.

Whenever he returned from hunting, he looked happy and calm, Lilith thought. Without a doubt he enjoyed the wilderness. His hair was tousled and his skin slightly tanned. The hunting skins that he wore were the perfect color to blend with his hair. She glanced at him surreptitiously through her fluttering eyelashes. Though she made every attempt to be avoid such feelings, her very being ached for him so.

2

A HANDFUL OF MOONS had passed since her daughter's womanhood ceremony. Hana, Lilith's mother, striding through the village, could not help but see that all of the young women who had been betrothed on that day were now married and one of them was clearly with child. Lilith, meanwhile, had become a shadow of herself, seldom eating her meals with enjoyment anymore. There was no question that her already trim body had shed flesh. At the family fire that evening, Hana observed her daughter's unusually quiet detachment. This was clearly not normal for her. It was difficult to know the proper thing to do now. All of this time had passed and her husband, the headman, did not appear to be rushing to make a decision regarding the suitors. In fact, he seemed to be unusually slow to discuss anything in reference to the issue. The ceremony had become a dimming memory. People had begun to wonder why no marriage announcement was yet forthcoming. Their usually exuberant daughter had begun to mope about. Her husband had said nothing, but perhaps he too saw Lilith's change in behavior. He was not the kind of father who would ignore a painful situation for his child. One of the traits that made her love him was the depth of the love he bore for his children.

Despite the advantages of political alliances to be cemented through marriage, his love for his daughter would cause him to want the best union for her personal happiness. The people of the river were a peaceful people, good neighbors to all around them, so there was little of serious threat to their safety. Hana decided that the talk of political concerns were more posturing than anything. She would speak to her husband tonight as they shared the sleeping mat. This situation must necessarily be resolved now.

But Lilith decided to take the matter upon her shoulders. After all it was her life at stake. She found her best opportunity that very evening at the family fire. "Baba?" Lilith spoke to her father, using the diminutive name she had used since childhood. The other members of the family were out of earshot. Her mother had retired to the mat. The younger brothers had been asleep for a short while. She had sat weaving, hoping for this chance.

"Yes, dear girl." He was extinguishing the fire and had been deep in thought.

"I do not want to speak out of turn, but my, I…, I…" she stopped short stuttering, obviously flustered.

Her father sensed that she was truly perplexed, an obedient daughter who had concern and wished to give him respect. He was hoping that part of the dilemma that had been shadowing his own thoughts for the past few days could be resolved.

"My daughter, I have been thinking that you did not seem to have any particular enthusiasm for those candidates who are pressing for your hand. It is most important to me that you have a good life. Tell me, is this not correct?"

"Baba, I do not wish...." she again paused carefully. "I do have a preference, but it does not seem that he chooses me."

"Lilith, I feel it is important to note that two people must be of one accord in order to build a life. Who is it that you prefer? Has he chosen someone else?"

"Baba, he and I have always been together. No other girl has ever been in his eye. He must prefer me. I just do not know what is in his mind now."

"Ahhh.." her father was now sure that his musings had been correct. She could only be referring to one person. "You mean Adaama, our lone hunter."

"Yes, Baba. Why would he not express himself like the others? He has always been at my side since we were children. It has never mattered to me that he was different. We have been companions since we were born."

"That is true. I realize that you see it so my dear. It is possible that his adventure was an attempt to pretend that the ceremonies were not occurring. It is important that I ask you if he has ever expressed himself privately. Or has he...?"

Before he finished his sentence, Lilith brought her head up sharply, "Baba, he has never done anything improper".

Her father assured her that the question he was asking was not meant to dishonor the young man, only to determine if he saw her as something other than a sister companion. He worried she had read something more into a relationship than was there. Men would be men. It was not unusual that young men did get out of hand. He knew that his daughter was not a silly girl, but she was still young, innocent and subject to misunderstanding this type of a situation. It would require very cautious handling to bring it to a satisfactory conclusion. He offered her some comfort as he bid her goodnight.

"My dear girl, you go to your mat now. Dream that your father will make every effort to see that you are given the match that you wish for."

Hana had lain quietly in the corner awaiting his retreat to the sleeping mat. She had satisfactorily listened to the conversation between her husband and daughter. Now she would not be forced to speak to him of this matter. She turned to her side and welcomed sleep. Perhaps now her daughter would have a chance to be happy. Hana's primary concern was that her daughter have the privilege of experiencing that special bond which occurs between two people who grow to love one another completely, as she had with the headman. They shared a good life. He was a wise and respected counselor, as well as a physically powerful man. They had produced magnificent offspring, two sons and this lovely daughter, the crowning glory of their lives.

The headman approached Adaama a few days later, asking his advice about hunting grounds. Everyone knew that the boy spent a great deal of time in the wilderness. Of course he had been called to task some moons ago, so he needed to be approached carefully. He made it a point to advise the reason for his original upbraiding. He then suggested that perhaps the boy could show him this area since Adaama had such success there previously. The boy was pleased to escape the leader's ire and agreed quickly. As he turned to go, the headman suggested that they include the boy's father in the hunting party. Since his father might enjoy the change from his usual fishing, it seemed a good idea and there was always some definite honor in being asked to hunt with the headman. Before dawn on the next morning, the three men set out for one of the grassy foothill areas east of the village where the game abounded in quantity and variety. It was an easy companionship and the day progressed well. Little effort was required because the game seemed to fall into their path. As they took a well-deserved midday rest in a shaded area, the conversation turned toward the activities of both families. The headman was cautious in his broach of the subject. It was reasonable that he would be concerned about them both because of his position. On a personal level, the two wives had become close and shared the births of their children. The children had, of course, become the best of friends. Common sorrow of the loss of Adaama's younger sister further cemented the bonds between the women. Eventually the talk turned to the recent coming of age ceremony in which Lilith had participated. The younger man became especially quiet. His father had asked if an announcement was soon to be made regarding Lilith's betrothal since a fair amount of time had passed.

"No, my friend. We seem to have a problem in the matter of my daughter's future." The headman shook his head in a defeated manner.

"What could you mean? I have been told that many suitors are interested in the hand of the most comely girl of the group!" Adaama's father laughed heartily.

"It is true that many have expressed interest. However, it seems that my daughter's heart is yearning in another direction." The headman spoke sincerely.

Adaama turned toward the headman, speaking quietly. "Whatever do you mean?"

"My son," he answered. "She seems to have feelings for you."

The boy turned his face away west toward the village, as if attempting to see some answer by looking toward home. It was true that he could not bear to think of her betrothal to some stranger. But somehow it was difficult to imagine their relationship being different. He knew that he had expected that she would always be a part of his life. One of the reasons that he had left on her ceremony day was his confusion about his feelings for her. She could have any suitor, he knew, and this too attributed to his questions. Why would she choose him? Lilith was the most popular girl in the village and in some respects, he was almost an outcast. Many did not accept him even now. He made the query aloud.

"Are you sure that I am her heart's desire? Could it merely be that I am the known factor?"

Her father blustered, "What do you mean that you are *known*?"

"Sir, I neither meant, nor have shown, disrespect. We have been close all our lives. I have loved her like a sister." The boy quickly put any possible fear over the girl's honor to rest. His own father's face showed that he too had fear. He asked a question of him.

"Son, the kind of love that you refer to can no longer have a place since she is not your blood sister. Do you think that your feelings have now changed to those of a grown man for a woman?"

The headman had a strange, uncomfortable feeling. While one could see that the boy cared for Lilith, some nagging emotion cautioned him. He listened carefully as Adaama replied. Even after all this time, Lilith's father thought, his pale countenance was still somewhat unsettling.

"Father," he stared into his own father's eyes, "I have considered the situation carefully. We are adults now. It would make sense that our feelings change." He turned to her father.

"I would be honored if she would actually consider me as a suitor." Adaama's certainty was that he liked the person he became when reflected in Lilith's eyes. A stronger, better person was shown there.

The headman's reply was measured, "Adaama, I believe that you are a good man and a good son. Are you sure about this? You must be sure. My daughter is the jewel of my life."

"Sir, I have thought about this matter greatly. I am certain," his face bore an expression of relief.

"Then let us complete the hunt. We have a celebratory feast to prepare for."

The small party continued their hunting activities in good spirits. The game was just as plentiful as they had hoped. The feast would be one of grand proportion. As they returned to the village it was agreed that the older men would call the wives to dress the game and report the good news. Because of the families' long relationship, Adaama would go to speak to Lilith alone for a short time. Young men and women only met formally during group activities. In this instance the parents were granting an unusual privilege. A small group of children saw the hunters coming and spread the news of their return. By the time they had actually reached the center of village, both families were among those greeting them.

Lilith had not been aware of the identity of the members of the hunting party with whom her father had departed. She was now a bit confused. Her father had said nothing else after their talk by the fire. Her confusion gave way to embarrassment when Adaama sought her out. Her chest felt as though it would burst. This was not his way. He was always just there.

"Greetings, Adaama. I did not know with whom my father had gone hunting? Did it go well?"

He guided her away from the crowd, toward the bluff overlooking the river at the closest point. He looked at her as they walked. She was so important to him. There was no question of her loveliness. It was time to make her aware.

"Yes, all went well, but not because it was a good hunt. Your father spoke to me."

Thump, thump, she felt the excitement trying to break its way out of her chest. What did this mean? Her voice came out in a half whisper.

"Of what did he speak?"

He took her hand in his, studying the vivid contrast of the dark and light skin tones. Other children had teased and ridiculed him because of the color of his skin, but she, alone, had never treated him differently. She had been his champion, from childhood forward. Adaama made an effort to fit in with the group because Lilith had always been there to encourage him in this endeavor. In order for him to comfortably play with the other children, Lilith had devised head coverings for protect his fair skin from the sun. His mother had been amazed and improved the design of the coverings. Eventually most of the people in the village had adapted some form of this headwear for daily use, since the merciless sun took its toll on all of them. Now, she was a beautiful, fearless woman and he could do well with her at his side.

"Lilith, is it true that I am the person that you prefer? You would look favorably upon me as your husband?"

Her breath seemed to fail her. She opened her mouth to speak and no sound came. All manner of images flashed through her head. Suddenly, inexplicably, she was afraid. Why now did fear arise? Why now, when this was what she most desired in her heart of hearts? Finally she was able to take a breath and speak, "No one else would serve as well, Adaama."

He put his hands on her shoulders and kissed her forehead. "Then it is settled."

3

THE FAMILIES HOSTED a sumptuous feast during which the betrothal announcement was made. Since the boy had not made a public expression of his interest, some few of the neighbors seemed to question the manner in which the engagement had occurred, but most were not totally surprised. The two had been inseparable for all their lives, causing the people of the village to easily accept the betrothal as the natural next step.

As it should be for the wedding of the daughter of the headman of the river people, guests began to arrive from near and far, well ahead of the date. Because of Lilith's combination of beauty, intelligence and family connection, she had attracted a wide group of suitors from both within and beyond the borders of her village. Curiosity stirred the imagination of the wagging tongues of gossip because as her father's only daughter, the possible richness of her dowry alone had drawn more suitors than most families dreamed of. While her father had secretly prayed that the sun and moon could cease movement in the heavens so that his blessed child could remain proud, strong and innocent forever, he knew that the time had come. Eventually, he had gladly forfeited the advantages of political alliances to allow her a genuine chance at happiness.

Hana's primary concern was that her daughter find happiness. Her twenty-year union had been remarkably blessed by love. She had grown up in a neighboring village and had come to this place after her wedding feast. Her husband had seen her while hunting with the men of his village and commenced to the rituals of courtship. She had been equally taken and found it hard to believe that it had all happened so perfectly. It had been a good life. The oldest son had taken a bride, but this was the wedding she looked forward to most. When her daughter was a wife they would share so much more. Since she had never had a sister, Hana looked forward to a kind of closeness that she had seen among the women in other families. Her husband's mother had unfortunately died prior to their marriage. His father had failed to take another wife, so she had felt a certain level of isolation in adapting to her new life. She had finally made a close friend when Adaama's mother came to live in a dwelling nearby. This union was a natural culmination of the long association of these two families.

4

THE SHORT TIME of engagement passed without incident. During this time, Lilith felt as though her life was perfect. All of the obstacles to her happiness had magically dissolved. He was truly hers. Like any bride to be, she spent her practical time weaving mats and cloth for use in her new home. These items contained intricate designs common among the people of the river. Her dreaming time was spent with her already settled friends, giggling about her future as a married woman. Both sets of proud parents were most helpful in the other preparations. Unlike some, this newlywed pair was to be given a dwelling of their very own. As daughter of the most important man in the village, this was her due.

Finally the time of the wedding feast arrived. The weather in their region had cooled significantly, allowing for comfortable traveling.

Fires were being kept throughout the days, as well as the evening. For several days, visitors arrived in the village of the river people. The neighboring tribes routinely joined one another for feasts and ceremonies. Any wedding was a major event, but that of a headman's daughter was among the most important social occasions that could happen. She was also his oldest child and could possibly be the next ruler of her people. No one wished to slight this family. In addition, her prospective mate was a source of interest to many, who had heard of people like him, but seldom had seen them grow to adulthood. Few could resist the possibility of seeing others from his family, perhaps not as pale as he, but nevertheless entertaining to behold. Rumor and excitement had spread through the entire region. The wagging tongues of gossip were busily abuzz. Added campsites had more than doubled the normal size of the village. Visitors had come from miles in either direction. Never had such a gathering been seen for a wedding in this village, or even the region.

On the day prior to the feast, several members of the groom's family arrived. His grandmother was borne in a covered litter by two of her sons and two grandsons, causing a great uproar. Only few had seen someone travel in the manner of a queen from distant foreign lands. She was very old and exceeding pale, much like Adaama. They brought gifts as representatives of the entire family. Included in the party were the sons' wives and an old man said to be the distant cousin, whose wife walked along with the others. But also riding in the litter was a small child that was said to be his grandchild.

This little girl was about three years old, plump, healthy and happy like other children in this village. Her skin, however, was paler than that of the old woman with whom she rode. Her grandparents had brought her from afar to visit the old woman in the hope of learning how to help the child, Eve, to survive. While they were visiting, the opportunity had arisen to attend the wedding. The couple gladly accompanied their kinsmen for yet another chance to help this child cope with the rigors of life in the savannah.

This little girl possessed skin that was as pink and smooth as hairless newborn animals. Her eyes were as reflective as the surface of the river that gave life to the village. People who came close to her often felt fearful gazing into the pale orbs, but found her countenance a pleasant sight because she seemed to smile and laugh constantly. It was apparent that she was not aware of her strangeness. Unlike the old woman, who was her distant cousin, the child's hair was exceedingly pale, like her skin. Its shade was even lighter than that of Adaama. Only the dried grasses that covered the lowlands could be compared in color.

When the families gathered for the evening meal, much additional excitement was stirred by the presence of the old lady and small child. Lilith thought that the child was an oddly pretty little thing. While she had no fear of producing such a child herself, it was good to see one brimming with normal childhood traits. There was, however, some other unsettling air about her that gave the betrothed woman a strange feeling. Lilith pushed it to the back of her mind.

Accompanied by her mother and two of the grandmothers of the tribe, Lilith began her wedding day with a ritual bath at the sacred place at the river. A sense of history walked along with the group on the well-trodden path. All of the women had followed this same path and they were distracted with the personal recollections of their own wedding ceremonies and indeed, their adult lives to this point. This walk had prefaced their marriages and those of the daughters who followed them. Each of them had harbored dreams that the daughters' lives would be better than their own. A daughter who married well was a great source of pride for a family. Even the lower caste family with a beautiful daughter could look to improve its lot.

Lilith's mother, Hana, had no worries on this day because her highborn daughter would be the most beautiful bride that the region had seen. Most important to her mother, she was now happy. Lilith had begun developing into a beautiful young woman of perfect form well before her first moon cycle. Her smooth, silken skin shared the amazing color of the rich reddish brown earth. Its tones seemed to embody the sun's warmth. Her large oval shaped eyes were like those of the young giraffe that frolicked nearby. The unusual aspect was their color, as Lilith's eyes were a rich dark blue of a more intense shade than even indigo dyes. Thick dark fringes of lash magnified their exquisite loveliness. Her body moved with the feline grace of the cats that roamed the nearby countryside. Because of her grace, strength and agility, her physical gifts were unequaled in the village. It was also noted that she was intuitive and kind hearted, wise beyond her years, a natural leader. Tall like her father, she stood a full head above most of her peers. Her beauty was beyond compare.

Much time was taken in the ritual of bathing the bride in the special pool. After cleansing, both her skin and hair were thoroughly anointed with scented oils. These oils were patiently and thoroughly massaged over every part of her body. Once the skin was anointed, her body was wound into a special piece of fabric. As with the skin, the scalp and hair were lovingly treated. Ivory combs were used to dress the hair into the patterns used for centuries. Often, the red clay mud of the river was used to provide additional dimension to the pattern, however today Lilith wore her long, dark mass of hair clean and free with only exquisite combs of ivory added. Once these activities were complete, the group returned to the village. Here she was dressed in the clothing and jewelry chosen for the occasion. In contrast to some others, Lilith wore a gown as pale as the intricately carved ivory jewelry adorning her slim throat and dangling from her ears. The creamy closely woven fabric draped her body with a gentle elegance. Her family had acquired the luxurious foreign fabric from an itinerant trader well in advance of this time. Since the dress would be worn for her wedding ceremony, any expense was justifiable. No other time in her life would be as important to her and the family as a whole.

The wedding occurred on this crisp and clear day. Even more beautiful than she had been on the day of her coming of age ceremony, the bride seemed to emanate a glow that exuded from her very being and surround the two of them. Despite his pale features, the groom was handsome and smiling. Everyone was certain that this would be a successful union. As the visitors departed, they took this positive feeling away with them.

Though the romantic side of their relationship had started out in a different manner, the couple was trying to adjust to married life. Throughout that first winter, from the outside, it seemed that they could not have been happier. The young husband had fallen into the normal rhythm of the daily life of married men in the village. The daily tasks assigned to the men, as well as the tasks of their personal life, took up his time. He knew that some of his friends envied his life. They saw the beautiful Lilith as the ideal mate and felt it strange that he had needed to be prompted to set upon this path. Adaama felt the new intimacy to be pleasant, but Lilith was now a full-blooded woman, eager to discover her own sensuality. She was equally happy taking the initiative with her husband, as following his lead. It was difficult for him to accept both her fondness for the superior position and her eager appetites. She could not understand why on occasion he did not just relax and enjoy her lead. It seemed right to her that they should be equal participants in every aspect of their marriage. Adaama felt that he needed control that was lost when she took such initiative. For him, the pleasures of the sleeping mat became excessive and overwhelming. He was reluctant to let himself be lost in the supple, shapely darkness that was Lilith. Perhaps because of his physical differences, he had not been as eager to embark upon that aspect of adult life. As boys do, his friends often speculated about the sexual possibilities of manhood. Adaama was never heard to do so. There were whispers about him because he tended to be solitary and seemed almost uninterested in the girls. Some of the nastiest gossip concerned his time spent in the wild. Did his preferences, perhaps, lean toward the beasts? Few took such whispered ugliness to heart. Because he had always spent a great deal of time with Lilith, not everyone questioned his masculinity. His present life was pleasant, but he wondered if other women were as aggressive as his new wife was turning out to be.

Their dear friends, Naaimi and Bhutu, had married shortly after their betrothal had been announced. This pair was already expecting a child. The couples spent a great deal of time together, often sharing meals or chores. It seemed to Lilith that children were coming all around her in a shower of procreation. In her own family even, her brother's wife had been huge with child when Lilith had married. The birth of her brother's child had occurred shortly afterward and Lilith had spent time in the birthing hut with her sister in law. This baby was a most delightful combination of her parents. He seemed to smile and gurgle constantly. Lilith found it hard to believe that she had actually witnessed this angelic child emerge from the young woman's body. As the months passed, she found it fascinating to watch the child's development. Her own maternal longings began to surface. She wondered why she had not yet begun to exhibit signs of being with child. The majority of the young married women of the village were nursing new infants. Some were expecting to give birth soon. She alone remained without child. Had she not strongly believed that her marriage to Adaama was going to one day be right, her spirit might have been less buoyant. Though he was still the same sweet boy that she had grown up with, she sometimes questioned the strength of the developing marriage. Lilith was thankful that her father had begun to occupy her time with the affairs of the village. The headman had made the decision that his oldest child would be the person whom he would instruct to succeed him as leader. She had always been the strongest and brightest of his offspring. Nothing had changed. Her marriage had only further illustrated her superiority since she had also proven herself to be completely capable in the womanly arts. This balance was essential for a female leader. This informal instruction proved to be the saving grace that kept her from becoming overly concerned when they had no child after the first year had passed. The headman found intense satisfaction in his daily encounters with his daughter though there was no urgent need for him to step down from his present role. It was, however, important to have someone ready to fill the role of leader when the time arrived. At times he was overcome with pride at her grasp of the machinations of politics and her skill in dealing with people. Not a single person in the village had questioned the choice of his daughter. She had become even more loved and respected by the people of the river. It seemed that her marriage to her childhood companion had further endeared her to them. These people valued loyalty above all. Despite his differences, Adaama was one of their own.

5

HANA RELAXED IN the cool dimness of her hut. The season was warmer than usual and she was beginning that time of her life that often had its own added warmth. One of the village women had brought a bowl of the herbs to help soothe her discomfort. She had steeped some in water and sipped the potion throughout the day. Her hands moved rapidly as she wove the reeds together to replace the family's sleeping mats for the approaching cold season. Weaving continued to offer her great satisfaction. The skill that she had developed over the years was both a comfort and a source of pride. Her work was valued throughout the region. Not only did she execute the traditional patterns, but capably created new patterns. Her daughter possessed the same natural abilities and time would surely show her talent to be equal. She looked up to happily see Lilith enter the hut with her father. It was still early in the day and Hana hoped that she had come to sit with her for a time. She knew that Adaama had gone on a longer hunt with some other young men. In such an instance, her daughter sometimes spent her time on the mat of her girlhood. On other occasions she might spend daylight time with her friend Naiimi. After the greeting, the younger woman picked up a handful of the reeds and joined her mother in weaving of the new mats. The two women looked up to a jingling noise and Hana was hit by a rushing bundle of energy. The sturdy little boy, Obi, had been born shortly after Lilith's marriage. He was such a busy, energetic child that his father had created miniature bells and attached them to a strap so that his every movement could be known. By then securing them to his rotund little middle, an adequate warning system was created. Her brother, the proud father of this adorable child had departed the village with the group of hunters. Obi and his mother now joined the women. He caused a temporary distraction as the hugs and kisses were shared with his *Yaya,* or grandmother, and his aunt. Lilith made every attempt to remain at some emotional distance, avoiding the painful thoughts of her own childlessness. This was even more difficult since her brother's wife was again with child. Lilith loved her family but was careful to maintain her boundaries. She needed to focus on all that was so right with her life. Her fingers flew nimbly through the reeds, creating the beautiful ancestral patterns to which they were accustomed. The women worked deep into the night. By this time the task of weaving mats had been completed, a sleepy Obi had fallen into complete unconsciousness in his grandfather's arms. The headman cherished this small male child above all others. He often mentioned to Hana that some special bond existed beyond that he had shared with his own sons. Everyone in the family was aware that he looked forward to the gift of other grandchildren.

On the following morning, Lilith rose early and walked to her friend Naiimi's hut. On this particular morning, she had felt as though her parent's space was too small. Her brother's small family had seemed to overwhelm her. She tried so hard not to feel out of place when they were around, but on this occasion she had been totally unsuccessful. The mere presence of the beautiful little boy caused an ache in her heart so palpable that she had found it difficult to concentrate. For some reason being with her friend did not cause the same restlessness. Since the two young women had been friends all their lives, Lilith felt safe and comfortable with her. For some reason, she did not feel resentful as she watched the expansion of Naiimi's tiny body. She sometimes felt that she was sharing the experience with her friend. Today she needed the comfort of her presence. From outside her friend's dwelling she noticed that the fire had not been started. After gathering the wood to get the fire going, she called out to Naiimi. Her voice sounded distressed when she answered Lilith.

"Please enter, my friend. I am slothful on this day. My body is not working with my mind." The young wife called out.

Lilith rushed in to see what the situation was, "Are you feeling badly again?" She asked.

"It seems to be a daily occurrence. The morning difficulties should have ceased by now. I am worried that my term is cursed."

Squeezing a dampened cloth and placing it on her friend's face, Lilith asked her if she needed to obtain assistance. "Should I go to get your mother?"

"No, I am sure that it will pass. Be very happy that you are not suffering so..." Naiimi saw the shadow that flitted across her friend's face and regretted her comment. She was very aware that her friend would gladly change places with her despite the problems attached.

"Just sit with me for awhile."

Lilith spent the better part of the day with her friend idling away the time in conversation. They rarely had the time for cheerful chatter and gossip as they had managed just one year before. Lilith spent so much of her time with her father tending to the affairs of the village that she sometimes felt that she neglected her friends. It was good to be able to spend a day like this.

"You should see Obi!" she exclaimed. "If your child is half as busy as he is, I am sure that you will look back fondly on these sick days."

"Eyeeii!" Her friend shrieked. "you are so right. I was at the river with his mother a few days past. She not only had the bells on him, but her own mother was there to help her. It does not help that she is again with child, however it does not seem to bother her at all."

"Some seem to handle it better than others. I believe that she is truly happy and somehow it does make a difference." Lilith glanced toward the door of the hut before she continued. "Why do you think that I have not …" She paused awkwardly. "I mean, everyone else.."

Her friend saw the troubled look on her face. "Lilith, Is everything proper? If so, don't worry. Surely you will soon be with child."

"But Naiimi, what is correct? I do love my husband. But...he…"

"What are you saying, my friend? Adaama chose you. Is there something wrong? Are things as they should be between you and he?"

Lilith lowered her voice even more and moved closer to her friend.

"I just feel that he is not as joyful about it all as he should be. Before we married, my brother said that some of the fellows felt that he … well, that he seemed to have no interest in girls. He is sweet and loving, but we are more like younger people playing. There is not enough.. passion." She burst into tears.

Naiimi was confused. They were young and healthy, such problems should only occur with those who were third wives. Even then the newer, younger wife often inspired tired flesh. She did not have any idea what the solution to her friend's problem was. In fact, she was not sure even what the actual problem was. She offered what little solace she could. Naiimi drew herself up to a sitting position on her mat, cradling her distended abdomen in her hands.

"Lilith, perhaps the wise old woman can give you something. It is said that she has answers."

"No, in my position, I could not go to seek such a thing. The wagging tongues would have my problems in every hut in the village before I could reach the circle of my own fire." She composed herself, drying her tears on the hem of her robe.

"But what will you do? "Naiimi touched her friend's shoulder.

"I will manage. It will get better. I should not have burdened you with this. It is my own to bear. Let us speak of lighter things. What names are you thinking of for this child? Did I hear *Agony* as a possibility?"

The two women nervously laughed and began to discuss names for the boy or girl to come.

6

DURING THE FOLLOWING season, Lilith became more involved in the processes of governing her people. More than once she was called upon to travel with her father. This time she joined her two oldest brothers and several of the elders making a visit to an adjoining province. As the journey progressed to the east, her eyes were constantly widened in amazement. Not only did she see plants, animals and trees that did not exist near the river, even the people were different. The villages were filled with people who were so unlike her own. Some had skin color of lighter shades than her people, but not as light as that of her husband. Manners of dressing their hair differed greatly, including the fact that many of the men wore hair on their faces. The style of dress was of fabrics, textures and hues unknown among her own people. Each day of travel opened to offer a wondrous amalgamation of sights and sounds. She found herself smiling continually. The experience was almost intoxicating. Never had she even imagined herself visiting foreign lands, nor had she thought that such places existed. She was thoroughly caught up in the adventure. During the journey, no thoughts of her personal life clouded her thoughts.

At the same time the small party of travelers created an equal amount of interest in their wake. Lilith's regal dark beauty attracted much more attention than the group could have imagined possible. The startling surprise of her dark blue eyes made her even more striking. As the lone female in the group, her presence seemed to confuse the people with whom they came in contact. Though the women of the river people held equal status with the men in their villages, most of the surrounding civilizations held women to lesser roles. Wives were little more than chattel. In these areas, decent women did not move about freely. More than once, her brothers had to correct negative assumptions about their sister's status. The fact that she was a woman traveling without her husband, caused a stir in several locations. In these places only prostitutes possessed such freedom. Lilith was quite capable of acting in her own defense and did so without concern for consequences. Rumors about her began to move ahead of the group. By the time that the emissaries reached the destination, the name of Lilith was on everyone's lips. Her beauty, her strength, her wisdom and her questionable status created a high level of interest among the eastern people. She was referred to as the 'Queen of the River people'. Whispers were rampant, with truth and fiction mingling freely with bits of gossip. Little did she and her people understand the degree of interest that they had raised among these strangers. Finally they were successful in an arrangement to meet the appropriate officials. After days of preparation and adherence to protocol, the agreements were made to establish trade routes. As the treaties were concluded, the expected social activities commenced. The local leaders felt compelled to bring forth a dazzling display of hospitality. During the next few days of feasting, the members of the little group were treated to food and drinks unlike any found in the simple fare of the river people. Fruit adorned cakes made from unfamiliar grains tickled the palates. Drinks made from fermented fruits were served in lavishly made vessels. Senses were heightened to unfamiliar levels. Lilith was the center of much attention from the local dignitaries. Several men paid her constant suit, not wishing to accept the fact that she was a married woman. Each failed to understand how a woman of such beauty could be allowed to travel alone. Unlike some previous encounters, no physical defense was required. These men were far more refined than any encountered before. Several watched from afar. In particular, a tall red-haired man stared at her for the entire evening. All masculine eyes were hers. The attention was as intoxicating as the drinks being served. Something inside her soul felt that she deserved the attention. But she stopped short of seriously considering partaking of the delights being whispered into her ears, since she loved the husband awaiting her at home.

The group began their journey home with high spirits. Many days had passed, the moon had moved through its phases one full time. Life in the village had moved along at the usual pace while the travelers were on their mission. When the group was sighted in the approach from the east, word began to pass through the village. A small group came forward to meet them as the morning sun reached its zenith. The cheery exchange of greetings and chatter helped speed up the final steps home. Various families came forward to joyfully claim their own. Laughing children were hoisted upon strong shoulders. Others were gathered up in embraces. Little Obi was running between his father and grandfather, bells jingling. His very pregnant mother smiled as she held to her husband's side. Hana gathered her second son to her after greeting her family members. Though the boy was tall and muscular, she felt that he was still too young to have been away from her for such a period. She had been plagued by nightmares for the entire time. Her husband, daughter and the two sons were too many to lose should there be some mishap. Now she could rest her mind. The family group slowly made the way to the hut of the headman where Hana had hastily laid out a sumptuous meal.

7

AMID THE CHAOTIC jubilance of the return, none of them had noticed that Lilith had slipped quietly away. As she trod the path to her own dwelling, Lilith's mind was filled with questions and dismay. Virtually everyone in the village had been there to greet the travelers. Adaama had not greeted her. In fact he was nowhere to be seen. After such a long absence, she could only hope that his joy to greet her was being contained in the privacy of their walls. Her heart began to sing, her steps became lighter as she walked in. She adjusted her eyes to the dim, cool interior. Each item was exactly as she had left it. Her spare possessions were in the proper order. The sleeping mat lay empty. Too quickly, it became apparent that her husband was not here either. Divesting herself of the burdens of her travels, she unfolded her weary body on the sleeping mat. Her disappointment took upon great weight, which seeped into her limbs and dragged her mind down into a numbing pool of blackness. As she slept, Lilith's mind repeated the steps of her journey. Feelings of amazement swirled in her head as people, places tumbled around in a swirl of color and sensation. She slept undisturbed as hours passed. Night had reached its halfway point by the time that she raised her head from the mat. Confused by the remnants of the dreams, her mouth was parched and for a moment, she could not recognize her surroundings. When it became clear that the walls surrounding her were her own, the question of her husband's presence again leaped to the forefront. Why hadn't he returned? She looked around her and a more comprehensive examination of her dwelling revealed the absence of his bows, knives and other hunting implements. At least there was a reasonable answer for his absence. She got up and poured a drink into her bowl. Alone in the darkness, the young woman sat and pondered the true state of her marriage. Why did she always seem to end up alone? Foremost in her thoughts was the constant attention that the foreign men had paid her. Why did her own husband seem to neglect her, when these men made such offers and promises? They certainly indicated that she was a desirable woman, not one to be left or ignored. Journeys could be dangerous in many ways. Her experiences, as well as her thoughts, were beginning to cause problems. As the faintest streaks of dawn began to show in the face of the sky, she began to drift back into slumber. Just as sleep was pulling her into a firm grasp, she felt a presence. Her eyes fluttered open to the sight of her husband standing silently next to the mat. He was utterly still and devoid of expression. The hunting gear had been put in the proper place and he had shed his clothing. As Lilith held her arms up to him, he took her hands firmly and pulled her to her feet. Gathering her into his arms, he spoke for the first time.

"I was not sure that you would return. It has been said that you took other mates while in the foreign land. Much time passed. I was not sure."

She replied without revealing her emotional turmoil. "But my husband, you were not here in our home when I returned. It was understood what my role was to be. I was in the bosom of my family and away only to serve our people. I have missed you greatly. "

His embrace was one of warmth and strength. The words were muffled as he spoke into her ear.

"I too have missed you. You must understand that when you are not here, I often feel lost. In the wilderness I feel less different, less apart. I lose myself tracking and stalking the kill. This time was even more difficult. There was much discussion among the people. Whispers were said loud enough for me to hear. A wandering trader came into the village from the east with much to be said about you. It seems that your name is on every breeze from here to the east as the beautiful Queen of the River people. I could not bear to hear some of the things that were being said."

Lilith felt as though something inside her had turned instantly hard. Tears sprang from her eyes. She had no idea such trouble was brewing back home. After the joyful experience that her journey had been, to have it made ugly was most disheartening. The decision to make the journey had been a sacrifice, since it was expected to be a hardship. While the outcome had been positive, that had not been clear at the onset. She had done this for the good of her people and yet here she stood defending herself.

"It was a difficult, but great and grand experience. I am sorry that you were subject to the sharp and wagging tongues of gossips. It is true that I was an object of curiosity and yes, also, great admiration, in that foreign land. Yet my only concern upon my return was to come to these walls, to be with you. Why do we spend time on this? Let us shut out this filth."

It was apparent that her husband had been as hurt as she was by the gossip. It needed to be wiped away from their ears and hearts. She gently drew him down to the mat. Her longing was pent up from both the absence and a new sense of her own personal strength. He held her tightly, then began to stroke her skin gently along the entire length of her body. Lilith felt a renewed sense of passion and hope. She entangled her hands into the bright locks of his hair as she hungrily brought his mouth down to hers. His response was vivid and quick as he found the center of her being. The joining of shadow and light was sweeter than any previous. He found himself deeply immersed in the rhythmic dance of lovemaking, for the first time without preoccupation. She found herself echoing his every movement, initiating movement. The act became something beyond itself. Finally this was what she had anticipated. In her soul she had known that this part of love should be filled with the joyous abandonment that she was now feeling. She was truly home. For the first time, she was truly home.

8

THE NEXT SEASON passed as though she was in a dream. Even the quality of the day's light felt magical to her. She seemed to breathe and move at another pace. Her feet seemed to glide across the earth as she made her way along the path to the river. Finally she had the glow usually observed on the newly married. Though her beauty had always presented a pleasant façade, the smiles on her face had changed. Anyone observing her noted that the smiles seemed turned inward. Her happiness was apparent and genuine. Some thought the travel in foreign lands had affected her in some manner. After all, much had been said about her adventures. Only her husband and best friend understood the true nature of Lilith's joy. When her moon cycle ceased, she first thought that it was a slight malfunction caused by the newly invigorated marital activities. She had given up thinking of motherhood and herself at the same time. Days passed into a third cycle of the moon and there was no question that she was with child. Her body began to exhibit the telltale signs of sensitivity, but unlike many others, she was never sick. Mornings were bright and glorious! Each morning she arose from her mat filled with joyous anticipation. Adaama often lay beside her simply to observe and share the glorious mood of her awakening. No complaints came from her about the changes in her body. If anything, she let him know, she felt like ripening fruit that she wished to generously share with him. The sweetly sensuous curves of her body were magnified to an even greater femininity and he gladly complied. It was strange to Lilith that she had witnessed her friend in such misery when her experience was anything but.

Naiimi had given birth to a girl during the diplomatic sojourn to the east. Sometime after the return home, Lilith had visited them. A delicate little girl lay in the protective arms of her dear friend. Naiimi seemed pleased, but subdued. Lilith failed to grasp the source of a certain darkness that she sensed riding the shoulders of the petite woman. She made a conscious effort to visit on most days during the course of tasks around the village. Her conversation was deliberately cheerful and filled with harmless bits of village news. Her own life was so satisfying that she felt pain for her friend. Bhutu did not seem to understand the difficulty Naiimi faced. He felt a sense of intrusion when her mother came daily to spend time with she and the baby. Talk circulated that he was considering taking a second wife. The wagging tongues of the village seemed to take pleasure in the family's troubles. But as quickly as it had begun, the clouds of discontent disappeared. Suddenly Naiimi rose from her mat, tied the child to her hip and resumed her life in the village. Tongues were stilled on that subject.

The time was growing near for the birth of Lilith and Adaama's child. The curve of her abdomen resembled the great bow that her husband often used for hunting. Her graceful sway and agility had not diminished. Beauty and desirability seemed to ooze from her person. The wagging tongues insisted that she must be under some good spell. Surely some good omen had been found in the foreign lands to cause such good fortune. As usual, Lilith's name was on every breath of the wind.

Her duties with her father did not have to take a back seat to her home life. Daily she made her trek through the huts to the river and back. Sharing kind words and smiles, she was as bright a presence as the African sunlight.

On the first day of the new moon in which her child was thought to be due, Lilith came to the birthing hut.

The old lady took one look at her and questioned her closely.

"Hello, my dear. Are you in pain?" The old lady saw no sign of distress on the younger woman's face, nor did she exhibit it in her carriage.

"The baby will come today." Lilith's smile was calm and sweetly sure of herself.

"Have you had signs? Surely you know the signs."

The old lady was beginning to be confused. This young woman was known to be intelligent, but had something happened to her mind? When women came here, they were usually clearly in pain. This one had placed one delicate hand on her stomach in a protective manner, but nothing else seemed amiss. She stood erectly with dignity. It did not seem that she could possibly be ready to give birth. It was her first child. Perhaps she was not as aware as some.

"I am sorry if you do not see the usual signs, dear woman. I do tell you that today is the day." Lilith continued to smile. "There is no real pain, but there is a heaviness that I did not feel previously."

The old woman thought that the headman's daughter was fooling herself. Perhaps she felt herself to be special and wanted extra attention. She had always seemed to be such a level headed person. Who knew how women would respond in these quarters? By the time that most women came here, they had enlisted family or friends. Often they were noisy and unruly. Since there was no one else here today and after all, she was who she was, the old woman decided to make no more objection. She had been here cleaning the quarters because several of the women were expected to give birth within this moon phase.

"Go ahead and sit down on the stool."

It wouldn't hurt to check her for progress. Just as the midwife was preparing to examine Lilith, Hana rushed in carrying the basket she had prepared for her daughter's journey here. The village tongues had observed her daughter entering the birthing hut and informed Hana. It had not occurred to Lilith to gather up anyone for assistance. Her husband was out hunting and the hut was but a short distance from the edge of the village. The space was allowed to provide some privacy for the women. Hana kissed her daughter's forehead.

"Are you having pain there?" she touched the small of her back.

"No, my dear mother. Do not worry. It is fine."

The midwife touched Lilith's private areas. She stopped quickly and looked up to Hana. A quizzical expression was stamped upon her brow.

"It seems as though the child is preparing to come very soon. She should be in pain."

Lilith made a motion to lean forward slightly. "You should attend to me."

Her mother was as confused as the midwife. She had borne her children without a great deal of effort, but at this stage she had not had the composure that her daughter was presently exhibiting. She sensed that Lilith was to be taken seriously. She quickly took out the special cloths that she had prepared for the birth. With little more than a sharp intake of breath, it happened. The midwife was barely able to catch the plump and perfect manchild. He began to cry without any prodding. As Hana took him for cleaning, she was overcome by the gravity of the moment. Her grandson was a beautiful little boy with dark hair curled past his ears. The rich warm gold of his skin was lighter than his mother's, but normal. Every detail of his body was perfect. He moved with strength and vigor. While the midwife completed the cleaning of the new mother and the birth chair, she continued to maintain her previous state of amazement. Never in all the years that she had tended this hut, had she seen such a thing. Young women often had to been carried from this chair sobbing. Lilith had easily moved herself to the mat once the afterbirth was expelled. She now almost sat erect holding her child. What was this young woman made of? The baby was normal, healthy but not extraordinarily small. She had barely made a noise when she expelled the baby from her body. Such behavior was often seen in older mothers who had given birth many times. Never had she seen such in a young first time mother. It was as though she had done it a hundred times before. Was this a blessing or a curse? There had been many tales about her journey. Who knew?

Lilith stared at her son. As these years had passed, she had grieved for a child.

Now it was done. Her perfectly beautiful son had come. He stared back at her unblinkingly. His large eyes were the darkly gray color of a stormy sky. The thick fringe of lash around them was black like those of his mother. He lay perfectly still. Everyone said that babies didn't see in the beginning. She no longer believed this. Her son's gaze was one of examination and acknowledgement. Her life was now complete. This small person in her arms made them a family. He moved his head slightly. In that instant she knew that he knew who she was. It was as though he was making a conscious decision about her as his mother. She touched the corner of his mouth lightly with the tip of her nail. A smile rippled across his face. The midwife gasped audibly.

"What in the name of the gods...?"

The old lady was visibly shaken. This day had been filled with too many strange happenings… A birth without pain… now a newborn child who smiled within an hour of birth. She looked around her and realized that she was the only one who seemed upset. Both Lilith and Hana wore expressions of serene contentment as the new mother suckled the babe easily.

Word of the birth had circulated throughout the village. The celebration had begun at the dwelling of the headman. The proud father had returned from his hunt only to be informed of the birth of his son. His initial reaction was subdued. His thought was one of thanks for the health of his wife and child. When Hana came to give direct news to the family, he found himself in awe at his wife's conduct. While Lilith had always possessed a great personal dignity, this was special even for her. This last year had brought an unexpected level of happiness to their union. Somehow the gossip had brought them closer together. Lilith had always been so, so above all things. As a child, she was the leader. She was best at everything the children did. As the beautiful daughter of the village's headman, she seemed almost too good. He had always loved her, but the adjustment to sexuality had been slow and tense. It had more to do with his personal insecurity than anything that she had ever done. He had never doubted that she loved him. At no time in their lives had she shown interest in any other young man in the village. Because of the charismatic nature of the young woman herself, as well as her family's position, everyone had wanted to know everything about Lilith. Even as a child, silly rumors floated about. Now as an adult woman, it had become vicious. Even he had listened for a moment to some of the tales coming back from the east. Though she was in the company of her father and brothers, still the tongues wagged. The gossip had proved her vulnerable to something. One of his problems in dealing with her had been her superiority. When she returned, he saw a different face. She had been hurt and needed him. By creating an emotional safe haven for her, he had found his own shelter. Now their child was here. For the entirety of his life, his coloring had put him so apart from everyone else. His differences had finally become lessened when he understood that his wife did love him and need him, despite any differences.

9

LILITH AND HER family thrived. Her son was developing into a sturdy, handsome boy. He was unusually beautiful, as well as unusually solemn. Even when straddling his mother's hip, he seemed older than other babies. Though he could be seen laughing with members of his family, the child presented a grave, emotionless face to all others. Both his parents doted upon him. Their love was reciprocated. The little family was undeniably happy.

Lilith continued to assist her father in the processes of governing the people. She spent her days moving about among the people. At times she offered assistance to young women learning the crafts and skills expected of them. Her craftsmanship had been honed over the years to a level of excellence. Even among the women of her people, her skills were considered superior. Her home was filled with examples of her baskets and mats that were both beautiful and exquisitely crafted. She enjoyed sharing her skills with others as her mother had done before her.

Hana's hands had begun to cause her pain in the last few years causing her to limit her weaving activities. Her grandchildren had become her primary interest. Beside Lilith's son, there was the boy, Obi and his sister to occupy her heart. Since the headman had his daughter to assist him in governing his people, he was able to spend more time at Hana's side. The youngest of their children had not yet taken a wife, but it was hoped that he might marry soon. He was smitten with the second daughter of the leader of the mountain people. The couple had wanted to marry but the girl was unable to take vows until her older sister had a husband. Her father had explained to the headman that his son could have the very special privilege of taking both sisters as wives. Despite his eloquent argument that the two girls came with double dowries of many goats, pigs and various other riches, neither of the young couple wished to share their union with her sweet, but homely, sister. However things had begun to look more promising. Recently, the father had received an inquiry from a widower from a neighboring lowland who was most eager to take a new wife immediately. He had been left with six children, the youngest of whom was still not weaned. His wife had taken a fever and died just within the last moon. Since his two oldest children were just barely old enough to help him in the fields, he was desperate to remarry. He assured the father that he needed a good girl who would work beside him and care for his children. He was not as concerned for her beauty outside as he was her heart. His reputation of being a good man had made it almost a certainty that the father would accept his proposal. This would clear the way for Hana's son to marry the girl he desired. She looked forward to this last marriage among her children even though it meant that she would probably lose her son. The mountain people also passed their leadership down through families and the girl's father wanted to groom her son to take that mantle. No one among his people had objections.

The cold season was fast approaching. Hana hoped that the wedding would occur before the snow set in. Any trails to the mountain villages could become treacherous if the weather took a nasty turn. It would be considered an affront if her family did not make the journey. She did not wish to become forced to spend the entire season in a strange village so far from home. It would not have been

such an inconvenience when she was younger. Indeed, it might even have been an adventure. Now she wished to be at her own home fire at all times. The rustle of feet startled her from her reverie. The headman walked briskly into the dwelling. A smile creased his face as he looked into her eyes. "Such a man," she thought. It continued to amaze Hana that the sight of him still stirred her to her core. He had always been a handsome man. The gods had given him the gift of a well-formed body and pleasant features. Time had improved upon, rather than taken away, his looks. He remained strong and vital even in their lovemaking. Nothing would have convinced her that at this stage of life, such fire would remain in her marriage bed. She rose to hold him in her arms.

"My husband, you appear to be bursting with news of some kind."

"Yes, a messenger has come from the mountains. The weddings will go forward as soon as we can arrange to be present. "

"What do you mean *weddings?*" she was slightly confused.

"Ah, yes. The family has decided that both girls should marry at the same time with one feast. It seems that the older girl is actually quite taken with her older suitor. It is turning out that despite his urgent circumstances, it is a love match. His wife had been ill since giving birth to the youngest. He had been alone for all that time and had been urged to take another wife for several seasons. The girl loves children and is happy to become an immediate mother to his brood. I hope that you will not be upset, but I sent one of our young men back with word that we will arrive three days hence. Since we knew that it could happen soon, I had made preparations for the family to travel. The messenger who came, can rest and will return with us. It is imperative that we make the proper impression."

Hana took his face in her hands.

"Have I ever doubted a decision that you have made? Your word is mine. I too, have been making ready to travel. In fact, this was on my mind as you arrived."

"How could I have even doubted you?" He laughed heartily as he hugged her tightly. "I have already spoken to the children. They and their families will be ready to leave in the morning. I questioned taking the babies, but since all are walking around now.." He trailed off.

"I am sure this will be a good journey. We agree that we must present a united front to support our son. It is good that we go quickly. I was thinking about the weather. Even though it is not that long a journey in decent weather, snow could make it very bad."

"My dear, I have spoken to the priests. They say that the skies will not produce snow for at least two moon cycles. You have not traveled to the mountains in a long while. You have forgotten the seasons there."

She had to agree. Once when they were very young, it had happened that they had become trapped in the very same village. As a young woman she had accompanied him on a journey. They had first established the friendship shared with these people. It had been pleasant enough, but the ever-present cold did not endear that area to her heart. Here near the river, life was not so hard. This journey and this blood tie to the mountain people could only strengthen them all. The entire region would remain a peaceful place to live.

10

N AIIMI LOOKED ACROSS the horizon as she worked at the
loom. Her talent for the cloth had developed immensely. As a
very young woman she had had little interest in the crafts practiced
by the women in the village. After the birth of her daughter, she had
discovered a need to have something of her own. She found solace in
the motions of the loom and satisfaction in the finished product. For
hours, she sat working the patterns of the cloth. Often her two daughters played at her feet as she worked. No one had ever discussed the
dark period she had experienced after her first daughter was born. She
realized that she had almost lost her husband. Perhaps, not lost completely, but certainly the addition of another wife would have changed
their lives. Even though he was her best friend in many ways, Bhutu
was a selfish man. When she lingered too long in the childbed, she

start

was not being a proper wife. Perhaps his small stature made him more eager to prove his manliness. The sense of humor he had always shown as a youth had begun to thin. He was no longer the quick, laughing boy she had loved. Behind the public face, was a man who struck her at the least provocation. Unlike her statuesque friend Lilith, Naiimi was a petite woman. Her delicate body made her the ideal match for a small man like Bhutu. At the same time, it had made her his easy prey. It was difficult for her to sometimes believe that it had come to this. She could never predict when his behavior might become violent. It was clear that it never happened when their daughters were present. He loved both his daughters. They were lovely, good-natured children of petite stature like their parents. At this point in her life the children were the center of the relationship. When others were about, all appeared to be as it had been. Naiimi was ashamed to discuss this with even Lilith strangely enough. Lilith had come to her when she had experienced bad times at the beginning of her marriage. She had not been ashamed to tell Naiimi about Adaama's reluctance to share her bed. Even though such a thing was seldom discussed, they were friends and it had not mattered. Naiimi sighed visibly as she thought. Lilith was brave. She had always been the fearless one among them. After all the troubles, she was now happy. When she had made the journey to the east with her father, the gossips of the village had been constantly busy. That a married woman would travel so far without her husband ...there had been whispers about Adaama... people heard things. He had never been like the other boys. So many of them would sneak to the dwelling of that woman outside the village. He had never been known to say or do anything out of order with any of the girls. Because Lilith was her friend, she did not discourage her interest in him when they were young. But then she also had not heard all the whispers at that time. Even though Adaama was his friend, Bhutu had eagerly told her the stories after they were married. He had often bragged that she was lucky to have him... that her friend Lilith wished she had such a man to warm her sleeping mat...that she had been heard crying, even begging Adaama for such favor. When they had produced no child early on, the stories were whispered around many fires. Bhutu made sure to bring them all home to her. He seemed to feel that telling her such stories could change her relationship with Lilith. Even when the couples spent time together as friends, he had found the need to say such things. She recalled one evening after they had shared the evening meal and had barely returned to their own walls. He had started in immediately.

"Such a strapping fellow my pale friend is... A good hunter... but the village wags say that he spends time in the wilderness rather than in his own dwelling. They say he must do it in the wild, with the animals, because his wife has been heard to beg him to do it with her at night."

Naaimi was hurt that he would repeat such filth about someone that she thought he considered his friend. Poor Adaama had always been the target of hurtful words when they were children. Lilith had been his defender. Since she was the perennial leader, the other kids eventually left him alone. It was too bad that the ugliness had never really gone away, just changed the shape. Since Lilith was her friend, the wagging tongues did not repeat those hurtful things to her that Bhutu dragged home like dirty little offerings. It was wonderful that her friend was now happy. After her return from the east, their marriage had changed. Then the birth of her son had seemed to complete her. He was a toddler now, a beautiful strange child...always so serious... Another child was on the way. Lilith had begun to show just the slightest body change. Her first childbearing had been so graceful. This time as well, she looked as lovely as she ever had in her life. It was almost impossible to understand how one woman could carry children with such grace while another suffered so. Her own experiences had been nothing short of nightmarish. Carrying the second child had been as difficult as the first. Her small frame seemed swollen and distended from the beginning. Bhutu was even more the braggart, forever beating on his chest about his potency. Of course he had been absolutely sure that it would be a son this time. But when the little girl had been born, he melted at the sight of her. Personally, Naiimi was thankful that it had been a girl. She did not want to give the world another tiny man who might end up a tyrannical idiot like his father. Bhutu found the need to try to control every part of their lives. He behaved like a man with a harem of women to please him. The girls did dote on him and she still made the effort to please him in order to prevent seeing his other face. He was, after all, a good provider and it could be worse. Naiimi had decided that she was resigned to her fate. She completed her weaving and pulled the frame and stool into her dwelling. The older girl was very helpful in assisting her mother to gather up the things. Bhutu would be in from the fields soon. She needed to prepare the evening meal quickly.

11

THE LITTLE BOY stood looking out at the two forks of the river. The bluff upon which he stood was the highest point in the area. Anyone observing him would have immediately feared for his safety. He had quietly slipped away from his family just to satisfy his curiosity. He knew that they would discover his absence soon and come to find him. He wondered how long it would take something to fall down to the water. He was an inquisitive child who wanted to know the how and why of everything. Even though his mother and father answered his questions, he knew which ones not to ask. He also knew which things they should not be allowed to see him do. The insects were a source of constant amusement to him. He would lie on his stomach and pull them apart. No one seemed to notice exactly what he was doing in such an intent manner. Now that the new baby was here, he had more time to himself. It was not an issue for him. He was not jealous of his tiny brother. He knew that his mother and father loved him. His place in their lives had simply changed. It was taking too long to grow up. The sound of his mother's voice came drifting on the wind. Hurriedly he rushed back to the place where he should have been.

Adaama saw his son running back from the edge of the outcropping. His heart caught in his throat at the sight. He then realized that the boy was deliberate and careful in his movement. Like his mother, the boy was physically nimble. Adaama himself was by no means awkward, so the child had inherited physical agility, as well as perfect stature. He was extremely well coordinated for a child of his age. Looking at him in the dappled afternoon sun, he looked like a miniature deity. The curling locks, his golden tan skin and his beautiful face did not seem human or ordinary. His father felt fearful for some reason other than his proximity to the bluff. It was obvious that he was in no danger of falling. He had moved away from the edge easily and ran toward his mother's voice. From the moment that he had lain his eyes on his first son, he had felt something odd. The boy's eyes had always been too deep. It was as though there was a very old soul inside this tiny baby. The new baby was nothing like his brother, who constantly gurgled and bubbled happily. Except that he seldom cried, he was a normal baby boy. His plump legs and arms were in constant motion. It was a joy to walk into the door and see his face. While the two boys had very similar features, they were so different from one another. He had never said this aloud to any person. Lilith would not have accepted such an observation in a kindly fashion. Her fierceness carried over into the defense of her sons. He loved his sons and did not want to be misunderstood. The last thing he needed was to destroy the peace in his home.

Lilith ran to the boy. She gathered him into her arms.

"Where did you go? I was so worried." She put both hands on his shoulders and looked at him. Nothing seemed amiss. Her son stood before her with no scratches, or sign of injury. He looked back at her without any childish rancor. At that moment he smiled an extraordinarily brilliant smile.

"Mama, I am so very sorry. I did not mean that you should be afraid for me."

He put one hand up to touch her face. Adaama walked up at that moment. He observed the charming scene for a moment, then put his arm around the both of them. The baby, who was strapped to his mother's hip, let out peals of laughter.

12

O N A LOVELY day in the following spring, Lilith realized that it had been too long since she had visited with Naiimi. Her mother and father had taken the boys and their cousins, so her morning was free. A nagging voice had urged her to walk in that direction on the day before, she had ignored it. When she came near the tidy little dwelling where her friend lived, something seemed amiss. Usually Naiimi sat outside with the loom on days as pleasant as this. The girls were not out about the entry. Lilith considered that perhaps she had gone to the river later than usual. As she came nearer the doorway, a groan came from inside. It did not feel exactly right. The cover was over the entry, and the windows... She called out a greeting and walked in. In the darkened space, she could barely discern the small form lying on the mat. As she moved closer, she saw that Naiimi was hurt. Her face bore a rainbow of bruises and cuts that were reddish, yellow and purple-y in color. When Lilith reached out to help, Naiimi raised her hands over her face in an attempt to cover the horrible sight, or shield herself from further injury. There were even bruises on her hands. It did not make sense. Only once had Lilith seen any woman marked up in such a manner. During her eastern journey, they had come across a woman lying in the streets. When she had attempted to help her, the woman had run away. Others nearby explained that she was a woman of ill repute whose former husband beat her whenever he happened to come into contact with her. The little delegation of river people found it hard to believe that such things happened in these cities. But this was here in her village and it was her friend. Lilith took cloths and a basin of water to clean the injuries as best she could. A quick trip to her own home yielded salves and herbs to create poultices. When she removed the bloody clothing from Naiimi's body, more ugly bruises were found. Some scars were older, faded and healed. By this time Lilith was certain that Bhutu must have been responsible. Her friend was barely conscious. The girls were nowhere to be found, but everything else was in order within the home. A rage began to build in Lilith. From her feet she felt an intense flush of heat rise to the very crown of her head. No one deserved to be treated in this manner, least of all, Naiimi. There was no way that she had ever made a noise to help herself because someone would have come to her aid quickly. If they had been afraid or unable to assist her, anyone would have known to summon Lilith or her father. Since her own children were accounted for, Lilith remained there for the rest of the day. She almost hoped that Bhutu would bring his sorry, sad little self in. She knew that she would have done the unseemly thing and raised her hand and a club to him. Luckily, he did not come home. When night fell, she again went to her own dwelling. After explaining to her husband what had happened to her friend, she returned to nursing duties. Adaama had been very understanding. He felt badly, both for Naiimi and for his wife who had to witness such ugliness. Lilith and Naiimi's friendship dated back as far as he could remember. Just as he and Lilith were a contrast in light and dark, Naiimi was her contrast in stature. The two figures could be seen together constantly... one petite, the other tall. His wife's friend was such a delicate person. It was hard for him to believe that the friend of his childhood could have done such a thing to her. Bhutu had always been a blustery little man. But he and Naiimi had been promised since they were children. Some believed that it had been a fateful circumstance since both ended up such small people. They had seemed so perfect together. He only hoped that his wife did not see the fellow at anytime soon. Never had he seen her that angry. She had been hurt and upset in the past, but this was beyond that. He discovered that Bhutu delivered his tiny daughters to his parents early that morning with the excuse that Naiimi was ill. Someone returning from a day's hunt had seen him leaving the village with enough supplies for a long journey.

For the next few days Lilith stayed to nurse her friend back to health. Once she became conscious, Naiimi was inconsolable. Despite the times that Bhutu had lost his temper in the past, she could not believe that he had hurt her so badly. Her despair was triggered more by shame than any other factor. Now too many people knew about the beatings that she had endured. She refused to leave the inside of her dwelling during the day. Once she was feeling well enough to perform her own chores, she went out well before dawn, or as late at night as possible. She became a wraith-like presence, avoiding as much human contact as possible. This horrid shame was a burden too weighty for her delicate frame to bear.

Eventually, the girls returned to live with their mother. Bhutu's parents at first made an attempt to shove the blame for his actions to Naiimi. They whispered about her poor performance as a wife and mother. After all most everyone remembered the dark period that she had suffered after the birth of her first child. She had not risen from her sleeping mat. What a disaster! Their son had been forced to threaten to acquire a second wife. He was always such a likeable fellow. No one had ever had anything bad to say about him. He must have been driven to do such a thing. Who knew what went on in the walls of a home? But none of the excuses could make anyone forget the damage that had been inflicted upon dainty, gentle natured Naiimi. Never in their village had anyone seen such violence. Glimpses of Bhutu's temper had surfaced and been seen by his peers many times over the years. Ultimately the reality of her injuries became the accepted truth. The village wags were silent for once. The tragedy was more than even they wished to deal with.

13

B HUTU HAD FLED along the footpath from the village to a main road. He knew that the community would not have accepted the injury he had done to his wife. It wasn't as though he had intended to hurt her. It had just happened. She never even tried to fight back, or cried out. She just put her hands up and cowered. Maybe if she had just fought back sometime. Oh well, it didn't matter now. He was going to find another life worthy of him. Perhaps in the foreign lands to the east there was a life waiting for him. He was a smart fellow, after all. Even though he had been a farmer, he also could carve things. He was good with the knife. Concealed in his pack were some teeth and tusks of ivory that would make combs and jewelry. He also had some good pieces of his finished work. With the time to do it, he could get better at the craft. Even the old carver in the village had always said that his work was among the best. This was going to be a better life. He would miss his daughters at first, but he was a young man and he could have another family. He would find a woman with some spirit. The traders who came to the village often shared the fires and told tales of the women in those lands. Vital mysterious women were out there in the east. He had heard that the lusty Anath women rode their men like horses.

"Ah, such women!" he thought. "What delights of the flesh they might provide."

He was sure that they would never allow themselves to be beaten! The village wags swore that Lilith rode her big pale husband in such a manner. And she had the nerve to hold herself in the manner of a queen. He had somehow always known there was something of the slut underneath that silky brown skin.

Many travelers were making the way along the eastern road. From time to time Bhutu walked along with a group that he encountered. Generally they were traders or men who, like he, were on their way to search for their fortune in the eastern cities. He heard many stories as the road passed beneath them. It was sure that he had done the right thing. Instead of rotting away in the village, he was on his way to better things. Whenever he had chosen to, Bhutu had always been able to show his charming side first. He seemed to be a pleasantly affable young man on his way to a better life. Nothing about him indicated that he had left his wife half dead in his home village. He was far away from home now. If he looked behind him, he could see the edges of his old world in the far distance. The mountains were the farthest place that just a few people in his village had been. He was now north and east of them, past the edge of the great gateway and proud that he had taken his life in his hands. It felt good to be his own man. The journey was a hard one, but he relied upon his skill as a hunter and followed the road. As the road lengthened he began to encounter a smaller number of travelers. There were fewer family groups and more harder looking fellows. At one point he felt it prudent to leave the road and avoid detection. The people began to look somewhat different. There were even more different styles of dress and hair. When the city came into view, he began to feel excited. Despite feeling very tired he was eager to begin his new life. At the edge of the city, he decided to seek out a place to rest. The people lived in odd places that seemed to be carved into the very mountainside. A friendly trader had gladly shared information about a place that offered lodging to travelers. Bhutu had been careful not to divulge any knowledge of his stash of ivory. Even though he was fresh from the outlands, he knew that dangers existed here. He was able to locate the lodgings by the landmarks that had been given to him. After securing a place to sleep and cleaning himself of the road, he went out into the town. His mouth was opened at every turn by the wonders of this place. At what seemed to be the center of the town, he entered an establishment offering food and drink. All manner of people seemed to be in this place. He was able to obtain what he needed. The trader had been happy to take a small portion of his carved ivory in exchange for the local tender. During the time on the road he had helped the young man understand how the system worked. Bhutu was not a stupid man in that regard and had quickly caught on. After enjoying a meal, he thought it smart to spend some time finding his way around the town. He knew that a part of the town was devoted to the trade of goods. Setting out from the eating establishment, he roamed through the town looking and trying to remember points of reference. Shortly before he reached the place of lodging, a slight shuffling sound caught his attention. As he turned to see what the noise could be, a pair of bandits suddenly fell upon him. He was punched and pummeled into unconsciousness. They continued to kick him until he bled from his mouth, nose and ears. As his body began to twitch, random thoughts were going through his subconscious mind. He had so many things to do. Where was he? Where was his father? He should never have hurt her.

When his mangled body was found the next morning, most of his teeth had been kicked out. He had bitten through his tongue with those that remained. One arm lay at an odd angle. Bhutu lay dead in this strange city. He had not managed to survive until sunrise. The trader who had been so nice to him was one of the crowd of people gathered in the early morning's light. Swelling had set in, rendering the body barely recognizable, but the kind older man remembered the slight, cocky young traveler. During his many years on the road he had seen the same story, time and again. He had made an effort to see that the young man came to no harm. He had enjoyed Bhutu's company and though he did not know the boy's name, he recalled that he was from the settlement of the river people. When he traveled that route in the following spring, he brought a small bundle of anonymous belongings and turned them over to the headman. Having claimed them from the innkeeper who knew him to be an honest man, the trader kept his promise. There was no question in the mind of Lilith's father. The items were easily identifiable. Each person who worked carving the ivory had a signature stroke. Just as the fabric clearly had come from Naiimi's loom, the carved items were from Bhutu's knife. He could not help but think that there was some justice in this life after all.

Naiimi had finally resumed her weaving. The solitary joy of drawing and combing the threads had become her only solace. Once her injuries had healed, she realized that Bhutu had gone away forever and that she was satisfied with his desertion. Never again would she allow a man to hold such power over her. Of everyone that she knew, he had seemed the least likely to hurt anyone. From the time that she was knee high, they were promised to one another. She had thought that he truly cared about her, but he had hurt her badly and left her alone.

Evidently there was some great allure attached to an abandoned young woman. As the time had passed, many a husband had crept to her door in the night. Each one believed her to be so desperately in need of male companionship that she would be willing to take any hyena who scavenged in the night. They gladly offered to provide what was needed, as long as she was willing to make no mention to anyone. It was a pathetic turn of events. She promptly decided that these men could not be trusted and refused them all. One, or two, came around who actually had the right to seek her out. Among them was a young widower who had lost his wife in the birth of their first child. While he seemed to be a sweet man, Naiimi was unable to feel the slightest interest. Another had come to the village from afar. He sought her out because his first wife had died and the flighty second wife was a toy that he had tired of. Even these legitimate suitors were rebuffed. The wagging tongues of the village saw and noted that by now at least one should have caught her fancy. They began to fear for her spirit. It was not healthy for such a young woman to turn away from life. And they had not seen any real display of emotion from her. What they saw, day after day, was her weaving in the sunshine.

On this day she sat in her usual spot, working diligently at a new pattern. When she spotted the headman walking toward her, it was clear to her from his expression that something serious had happened. First she worried that it concerned Lilith, because most mornings she was with him. But it was earlier than they usually could be seen traversing the village... Silently, he stood in front of her loom and handed the bundle to her. It took a moment for her to realize what it represented. She tried not to think about her husband anymore. Of course she recognized the piece of fabric. As she unfolded it, the contents spilled out onto the earth. Though it was obvious that the carved pieces of ivory represented some value, her first response was to cast them as far from her as possible. Bhutu had been purged from her heart, her home and mind. This intrusion was unwelcome. She realized then that he was dead. The headman told her the details quietly and quickly. He gathered up the pieces and assured her that he could dispose of them for her if she chose. She agreed with a nod of her head. When he left, she sat in the very same position as the sun changed its place in the sky. She made no sound. As the sun began to set, Lilith came running to her side. Her family had just returned from visiting the youngest brother in the mountains. His wife had given birth to their first child. When her father gave her the news, she only had to look at Adaama to explain her task. Kneeling beside Naiimi, she gathered her into her arms, only then did the widow let out a keening wail heard from one end of the village to the other. Only then, in the arms of her best friend, did she allow the tears to flow.

14

MORE AND MORE, the tasks of governing the village fell
to Lilith. Her mother had become ill during the winter and
the headman devoted his energy to the care of his wife. The older
women of the village made many an attempt to assist him in this endeavor, but he would not accept such aid. Hana was his beloved mate
and nothing could come between them in life. He was determined
to nurse her back to health. His family did not try to interfere in his
efforts because they understood since even they had never come between the two. When they were children, it was understood that no
wedges could be driven between Mama and Baba. This union served
as the model for each of them in forming their own marital bonds.
The marriage of their parents was a physical and spiritual success that
continued to endure. Each of them expected no less of their own re-

lationships. To their pleasure, Hana recovered completely during the following season. As she tended to the needs of her people, Lilith found great satisfaction in being at the center of the village's activity. She felt the village pulse as though it were a living thing. The ebb and flow of life never ceased to amaze her. It delighted her to see the births, watch the children grow and pause to talk to the old people. Every age group knew and recognized her as the person who stood next to the headman in governing them. Trade and commerce had developed just enough to help the river people to create a thriving economy. Lilith was instrumental in maintaining these essential relationships. Her many travels supported her people. She was a woman who, unlike others of her time, moved among men. Despite this, her husband and sons were primary to her happiness. The boys were growing up rapidly. They continued to exhibit sharply divergent personalities. Her youngest was all sunshine and smiles and his father's favorite. Lilith had loved to stand over his basket in the morning to anticipate his waking. He never failed to wake up with a smile on his face. Asmodo, her beautiful oldest boy, remained eerily serious and detached with everyone but his family. His intelligence was matched by his emotional distance. His mother refused to even consider that he lacked something vital in his makeup. Adaama watched his sons growing up and had begun to feel less important in the scheme of the family day to day life. It was obvious to him that Lilith was completely immersed in the affairs of the village, but did not seem to see that there was a problem with their son. He saw that the boy was left to his own devices a great deal. Strange things seemed to occur when he was around. He loved his brother and looked after him, but the same could not be said for other children. A little boy who fought with the baby boy ended up with a broken arm and was oddly silent afterward about the incident. Asmodo was, however, becoming an unusually fine hunter for one so young. His skill was improving so rapidly that it was becoming uncomfortable to encourage him. There was an instinctual sense of cunning in the boy. His uncles bragged about his prowess, but his father saw some other darker possibilities. Since Bhutu had gone and subsequently died, Adaama had developed no other close friendships. Even though he enjoyed a degree of camaraderie with his brothers in law, he often felt as isolated as he had as a child. Lilith seemed to becoming more self-sufficient daily. Her importance to the village often frustrated any effort toward privacy. He, in turn, had begun to spend more and more time alone in the wilderness.

15

ANOTHER IMPORTANT CONSTANT remained in Lilith's life. Her friendship with Naaimi was closer to that of sisters than anything else. Since neither of them had ever had a blood sister, each had filled some void in the other's life. Naaimi had no one else but her daughters, now that her mother had died. She continued to ignore all suitors. The people saw a lovely petite woman and still failed to understand her state of mind. Her oldest girl was rapidly approaching young womanhood and something primal in her mother wanted to freeze her development. Her fear was that her daughters might attract the same kind of man that their father had been. She knew that if anyone did to her daughter what had been done to her, she would kill them. There was no question or other consideration. She would kill him without thought to consequence. She was no longer the helpless, shamed girl whom Bhutu had beaten. As the mother of sons, Lilith's concerns were different. In fact, she had few concerns. As far as it went, her life was perfect. She had a husband whom she loved, the gorgeous boys, a wonderful primary family and a sister friend to count on. From time to time Naiimi had traveled with Lilith on a shortened mission of diplomacy. Her skills at the loom had inspired her toward improvement. By traveling to other places she had been able to see how people in those other lands lived and used cloth. Some of the things that she witnessed caused her particular dismay. The women in eastern lands were far less free than those of the river. They could not live alone without bother as she did. The foreigners had become accustomed to the river people coming from the south with their women ambassadors. Though the citizens had initially found it strange that these women were not prostitutes, it had been made clear to them. Naiimi now understood what Lilith had faced all these years. The rumors had drifting back home had been fueled by the local disbelief that such a beautiful woman could be more than a vessel for the use of men. She had certainly become adept at defending herself after living alone. The men in her village seemed to understand her refusals more quickly after she acquired skill with a knife. Since she was not as physically strong as Lilith, she had learned to use stealth. By placing the blade correctly in her robes, she could flash it in the speed of a spoken refusal. One stubborn man wore a scar that he claimed to have received at the hands of some nasty stranger caught lurking near the river. Seeing him caused her to be extremely pleased with herself. Only she and Lilith knew the truth. She wondered what the wags would have said had they known the truth about that. Those wagging tongues usually seemed to know everything that occurred by sunlight or moonlight. Their web extended far past the borders of the village thanks to the numerous traders who visited the river people. For these traders, gossip was as much a part of the stock in trade as the supply of

real goods. Information was passed to neighboring villages and far cities. It truly amazed her that some version of her experiences in foreign
lands was often recounted to her when she came back home. The two
friends shared laughter and tears over the things they learned about
their own exploits from the people of the village.

16

THE FESTIVALS THAT celebrated the summer solstice were an important event in the lives of every tribe and settlement along the river. In the towns and cities, the structure of these celebrations had changed shape somewhat. Family gatherings were often timed to coincide with these celebrations of life's bounty. So it happened that Adaama took his family to a far village at the edge of the great desert. There was to be a gathering of his relatives to celebrate the birthday of his grandmother, who was said to be nearly one hundred years old. Lilith eagerly undertook the burden of this journey. Since her marriage almost ten summers past, there had been little contact with his extended family. The group traveling included both sets of parents, their own sons and her nephew, Obi. The boys embarked upon the trip as an adventure. For the older adults, it was an opportunity to renew ties and enjoy the fellowship of family. By departing in the early hours before dawn, the travel was easier. They were able to make significant progress before the sun reached its zenith. At midday, time was taken to refresh themselves, water the pack animals and replenish supplies. When the evening cooled, the group continued along their way. After several days, the journey was completed. When they arrived at the campsite in the early evening, a carnival-like atmosphere greeted them. Tents had been erected in order to house the many visiting families. Oxen, goats, camels, donkeys and horses were tethered in a nearby area causing a dissonant chorus of bleats, neighs and brays. Feathered creatures of various types crisscrossed through the feet of the crowd. Someplace nearby, a band of musicians could be heard. Laughing children merrily pursued one another in spirited games of chase. As the adults barely settled themselves in, the boys were off and about with a gang of youngsters.

A distant cousin had promptly welcomed them and directed the group to prepared lodgings. The entire occasion was carefully organized and orchestrated. More than four hundred people of varying degrees of relationship had gathered to honor the matriarch of this clan. Lilith had never seen a group of this size. Even in comparison to her many travels, this was a momentous occasion. Many members of Adaama's clan had attended the festivities surrounding their marriage. This was a wonderful opportunity for the children to meet other family members. Because of the distances and difficulties often facing travel, scattered large families were blessed to gather once in a decade. During that evening's meal, acquaintances were made with a huge number of Adaama's uncles, aunts, nieces, nephews and cousins. Lilith made sure that she kept the correct affiliations in her mind. Some of the closer ones were simple enough to remember. One of his aunts looked to be a twin to his mother. In another case, there was an actual set of twin cousins who were easy enough to spot. She had always possessed the ability to effectively deal with people. In a gathering such as this, all of her diplomatic experience came into good use. Her father found the opportunity to reacquaint himself with numerous men with whom he had dealt over the years. There were hunting parties, as well as sporting contests among the younger men. Women gathered themselves into the tents for preparation of dishes for the large communal meals. They traded family news, gossip and homemaking hints. Babies found their way from arm to friendly arm. Children put themselves together into groups by sex and age. The exhilaration and good will generated by such a divergent group of people brought together by blood ties, was enormous. The days passed by in a lovely blur. As the tents were being struck on the final day, a group of adolescent girls gathered in the midst of the frenzied activity. Lilith stood with a few others quietly observing in the early morning sunlight.

A drummer struck a rhythmic beat and the young women began to answer with the lovely melodic ring of bells. From somewhere in the makeshift camp the distant reedy sound of a reed-like pipe joined in. A few other musicians and drummers converged upon the space. The girls slowly began to dance. In their midst, stood a girl of perhaps thirteen summers. She was slight, but taller than the others and swaddled almost head to toe. Only the top of her face could be seen clearly. The brightly covered scarves covering her began to swirl as she danced. Lilith could see that this was the girl she had heard about. This distant young cousin of her husband's, who had come to her wedding. Her pale skin was visible about her eyes, and on her hands as she jingled the tambourine. The eyes were as brightly pale as the morning sky. She danced with grace and inhibition. Her protective clothing should have restricted the movement of her willowy limbs, but instead it lent an odd degree of sinuosity. A heavily carved chain of silver glinted from near her feet. The attached bells jangled as the colorless skin of her ankles flashed from the hem of her robes. As she twirled with the volume and cadence of the music, braids swung out from beneath the scarves covering her head. Flashing about her face, her hair reminded Lilith of sheaves of grain ripening in the sun. The darker woman had become thoroughly accustomed to her husband's pale skin, but this girl was unnerving. She suddenly remembered the first time that she had seen this child. Eve was her name, and she had been three years old at the wedding. An azure scarf came loose and fell from the girl's face and Lilith saw that she was even more lovely than she had been as a child. The fine line of her brow topped the sweep of sandy lashes accentuating those sky colored eyes. The regal triangle of her nose flowed smoothly into lips that curved sweetly into a bow shape. The full lower lip was a soft rose pout. Along her cheekbones skimmed the blush of dawn. Her face held the self satisfied look of someone who knew a secret. Finally Lilith expelled the breath that she had been holding. At that moment, she looked across the space of the crowd and saw her husband. Adaama stood behind his father, near the drummer who had begun the impromptu chorus. His eyes were fixed on the girl. Across his flushed face was splashed a look that she had seldom seen. The yearning look was one of extreme astonishment, coupled with desire. He quickly turned away and walked through to the back of the crowd. Lilith felt as though she had been hit between her breasts with a giant stone. A physical pain throbbed in her chest. There was no question about the expression that she had read on Adaama's face.

The gathering at the center of the camp had dispersed. Most of the observers had returned to the task of preparing to leave the encampment. Oxen, camels and donkeys were loaded, hitched and packed. Families lucky enough to have horses had them saddled. Some groups were already departing the area. Despite the buzz of activity around her, Lilith stood motionless in the same spot amid the swirling clouds of dust. Rivulets of tears coursed through the fine coating of dust on her face. Why no one noticed her, was a mystery. Eventually, she wiped her face with the hem of her robe and went to locate her family. They needed to go, now. Easily she found the entire group, gathered, waiting for her.

"Where were you, my dear? …last goodbyes to say? "Her mother in law came to her. "Did you enjoy this occasion? I find it hard to believe that my mother still possesses such energy. We were gathered in her tent and I looked for you."

Lilith had composed herself as she approached them, but continued to be somewhat shaken.

"Oh, I do apologize. The boys had been near the animals. I went in that direction."

She glanced at her husband. He stood leaning against the pack animals. His face was expressionless. Evidently he had recovered, but she had not done so. A lump of pain and disappointment sat inside her breast. Her face was frozen from the pain. It was necessary that she appear normal.

"Are we ready to go?"

Her father stepped toward Adaama. "Son, the morning is getting away from us. Shall we move out?"

"Yes, all is in place." His words were crisp. He led the animals out. The group fell into place and began the trek home. There were at least four hours of travel possible on this morning. Both Lilith and her husband were quiet. Luckily, the whole group was less talkative. The journey was uneventful and easier than the original. When the tired group of travelers made their way back to the comfort and safety of the village, they dispersed to the respective dwellings. Only Hana saw that something did not sit properly with her daughter. As a mother, she unfailingly sensed danger to her offspring. Something was not quite right in the set of Lilith's shoulders, as well as in her eyes. She could not begin to fathom the storm that lay ahead.

By the time that the family had unpacked, it was time to eat the evening meal. Lilith prepared the meal as usual. The boys bubbled on excitedly about their adventures. Both mother and father primarily ate in silence. They replied in monosyllables to their sons' inquiries. Neither addressed any remark to the other. Even the children sensed some stiffness. Adaama was very simply removed from his surroundings. His eyes bore a vacant, distracted stare. His wife made an effort to appear oblivious, but she was acutely aware of his emotional absence. The only hope that she had was distance. The precocious girl lived elsewhere. Every fiber of her being prayed that the intensity of Adaama's reaction would dissipate with time, that it was the shock more than anything. Yes, the girl was beautiful. But more than that, she was like him, his very match. It was almost as though he had looked into a mirror and seen himself as a female. It made sense that he was shocked. After all he had never seen a nubile female who was like himself. His grandmother couldn't be counted. His mother was only a lighter brown color, like the spices that they brought from the east. None of the women in the family, in his generation, were like him. His own sister had not survived. Perhaps seeing that girl would not have been so much of a shock to his system if he had been exposed to females who looked like him. He was, after all, a man first. Besides they had been married for a long time. Men often react to very young women. Lilith kept telling herself these things over and over. Any answer would serve to try and calm her fear…any answer. As they retired to the sleeping mats, the couple barely acknowledged one another. Each was polite to the other, but any accidental touch was coupled with immediate withdrawal of the offending limb. Tension crackled in the air, but each pretended to be unaware of it. Sleep was hard won, despite the tiredness of their bodies.

When Lilith awoke the next morning, she was alone. The hunting gear was not in its place. Her first response was to look to see if he had taken the boy with him. Asmodo was asleep in the usual place on his mat. The boy loved hunting and most times accompanied his father. Even though he didn't always take the boy, today it mattered to her.

The day passed quickly. There were so many things to catch up on in the village. She visited with her brother's family. It was a pleasure to tell Obi's mother what a good boy he had been on the trip. Even though she was sure that Hana had already done so, it seemed only right to follow up. After a short visit there, she took the path through the village to visit Naiimi. Her friend sat pulling the threads of her loom. Lilith made a conscious effort to cast aside the pall of anxiety that covered her. Somehow she did not feel it possible to put her problems on the shoulders of her friend. They had shared so many hurts over the years. Today was different. She was determined to bear this burden alone. Her friend had seen enough ugliness. As Lilith walked toward her, Naiimi did not require a word to know. She saw the pain crouching all about her friend's shoulders. Lilith's attempt to mask her feelings did not escape her best friend. Naiimi's immediate thought was to query why after all these years, did Lilith think that she could hide anything? It was going to be a thorny task to get her to talk about it, but she had to do it. Over the years, Lilith had been responsible for saving her too many times.

"Welcome back." Naiimi decided to plunge forward. "How did you find the journey?"

The reply was careful. "It was quite eventful. So many people were there from a wide area. There were even more than at my wedding. You know the grandmother is near one hundred years old. Adaama's mother is the youngest of her children and he was the second to last child born to his mother. Only one other came to term, but she died before she could walk. His mother always seemed so distant. I believe that she had suffered so much loss, that she was afraid to be too close." Lilith babbled on and on. She went into great detail about the celebration, the relatives, the food.

Naiimi listened patiently, understanding even more clearly that something was greatly wrong. She allowed her to complete her prolonged speech. When she finally seemed to run out of words, Naiimi asked her directly.

"What happened, Lilith?"

Those large doe-like eyes quickly brimmed with tears. The indigo depths had become a stormy sea, shedding its surface. Naiimi got up and took her arm, leading her inside so that they could speak privately. The ears and eyes were everywhere. When she was able to speak calmly, Lilith began to speak slowly.

"It was the last day. There was this girl."

Her words made no sense to Naiimi. Adaama had no real interest in women. She didn't mean it that way. But he had never shown any interest in anyone else. Naiimi forced her attention back to Lilith's words.

"They danced and it was impossible for even me to take my eyes off of her. She was so exotic and beautiful. When I saw him, he had this expression on his face...this expression of lust and yearning..."

She collapsed into tears. Then as quickly as she had lost all control, she regained it. Nothing was to be accomplished in this manner.

"I am so sorry. I don't know what came over me. It is ridiculous to worry about this anymore. She was just a girl and she is far away now. His interest can be understood. When he returns tonight, I will make an effort to make him forget. We have been busy. It is going to be different now. We have our sons and we are not children anymore."

Naiimi felt that she could hardly say anything as she had had no success with men in her life. She saw Lilith compose herself and rise to leave.

"I am going to prepare the sweet honey cakes that he likes so. In fact, tonight I will prepare all of his favorite dishes..."

When her friend had departed, Naiimi returned to pulling the threads. She could not imagine the pain that was in Lilith's heart. Adaama had always been at the center of her life.

In Lilith's dwelling, one dish after another was prepared. The small space was a hive of activity. Lilith cut, mashed and ground the afternoon away. By the time of twilight, a chorus of wonderful smells wafted from the doorway. Arriving from play, the boys were convinced that some special feast was going to occur. From a distance the smells had come wafting out to greet them. Their mother always fed them well, but this was to be a step above the normal fare. Lilith greeted them cheerily, assuring them that it was no special feast and that as soon as their father returned the family would eat to their heart's content. They waited anxiously for his return. They waited. As the time passed, it was clear that their father was not going to return that evening. Finally, the three of them sat and ate. Despite the wonderful food the children recognized their mother's state of mind. She hardly touched the food herself. What she did chew upon tasted leather-like in her mouth. Her eyes kept looking toward the door. She actually went to bed at the same time that she demanded that the boys go to their mats.

When the morning came, there was still no sign of Adaama. It was not unusual that he went hunting for prolonged periods. Most often, others accompanied him. Asmodo, as well as Lilith's brother and his son were his usual companions. But this time, he had said nothing to indicate that he was leaving. In fact, he had been in a trance-like state since the morning at the campsite. Lilith threw herself into the affairs of the village. Many days passed and still he did not return. Only Lilith and Naiimi found any real significance in his absence. The people were accustomed to his hunting trips. If the truth were to be told, few men in the village had the level of prowess that he had acquired. An entire phase of the moon had occurred before Adaama returned. He was thinner, unkempt and even feverish. The sun had burned his skin badly. Shocked by his appearance, Lilith rushed to his side. Never had he allowed himself to be burned so badly. No words were exchanged when she observed his agony. She prepared the salves and potions to ease the fiery pain. His lips were cracked and blistered. Areas of his arms had blistered over the original burns, creating two layers of burned skin as though he had deliberately punished himself. For several days, he lay listlessly in the hut as Lilith worked to heal his burns.

No words passed between them about the journey, or his subsequent absence. The relationship had changed subtly. As a couple, they cared for one another and their rapidly growing sons. As a couple, they were friends, not lovers. There was tenderness, but not passion.

The girl was in both of their heads. Lilith knew that she was no longer what he desired. The specter of the pale, lovely girl hovered over their marriage bed. At times Lilith felt such strong physical desire that she came close to forcing the issue of intimacy, reminding her of the early days of their marriage. At that time, however, she had no idea that someone else might exist who could be a mate that he desired more. Now, the image of the girl who looked like him haunted her every thought.

Adaama had tried to push the girl from his mind. During his sojourn in the wild he had consciously fought to purge the vision of her face, her enchanting dance. He tried to put himself in the place of his wife. Somehow he could swear that she knew. It was unnerving, although nothing had been said. She seemed to know what he had experienced. It did not occur to him that she had seen him in the throes of his encounter. He presumed that she was just being her usual superior self. She was always the adult, even when they were children. He felt that he had committed some adolescent transgression. Never in his life had he done the silly things that other boys did. None of the sexual hi-jinks... no trips to the women who lived at the edge of the village. Perhaps he had been slow to mature, he now wondered. Even though Lilith had always been the object of his affection. He had not dared to desire her until they shared the marriage bed. Even then it had been difficult for him to change his feelings. But nothing in his life prepared him for the assault upon his senses that he had suffered at the campground on that early morning. He had wanted to touch and caress the girl then and there, to make love to her, to ravage her. Her mouth seemed to be beckoning his own. His head swam with the possibilities of the pale willowy body hidden beneath the jewel colored robes...the soft, subtle coloring... the sky colored eyes. He imagined that the tips of her breasts were the same rosy shade as her lower lip. It was as though she were created distinctly for him. Angrily he attempted to remove all thoughts of her from his head. She was little more than a child. Demons must be in possession of his mind. He knew who she was, the granddaughter of his grandmother's cousin. True, the relationship was distant, but they obviously had inherited the same condition from the shared bloodline. He had never before thought of his condition as being synonymous with beauty. For his life's entirety he had seen himself as unnatural and ungainly. Now he knew differently and his mind could not rest.

17

EVENTUALLY, THE COUPLE managed to salvage the intimate side of their marriage. As the months then years, rolled by, memories of the lovely, pale girl receded to edges of memory. For Adaama, she was a dream finally now dissipated. Lilith felt as though she had wakened from a nightmare. Their lives returned to the state that had existed before the trip. Day by day the routines associated with parenting created rhythms that both succumbed to. Concerns for Asmodo began to consume his parents every waking thought. Slowly it had become apparent that the boy enjoyed killing and even hurting things. Not another village boy of any age would dare challenge him for any reason. He had become as skilled at tracking and hunting as any full grown man in the village. His prowess in hand combat was becoming legendary. In one incident he had crippled a much older boy who was foolish enough to challenge him. His response to his parents' questions were matter of fact and apathetic. They were unsure what to do, because like many adolescent boys, their son appeared to ignore their considerations.

His extraordinary good looks and physical development were an additional source of dismay, attracting the attention of girls and boys much older than he. In every case, he seemed to be the controlling factor in the relationships. Like his mother, he was a leader. His influence, however, did not ever appear to be benign.

In the morning's mists, a group of young men were lounging on the rocky outcropping near the river, filled with youthful exuberance, laughing and wrestling. As she approached the area, Lilith did not feel particularly comfortable. At few times in her life had she ever felt as uneasy as this situation was beginning to make her feel. She fixed a firmer grasp on the reed basket of clothing, making sure that the angle of her chin did not betray her discomfort with the situation at hand. It had become apparent that those standing closest to her were strangers. From time to time groups of travelers made their way through the village. Usually they were no more than three people. Occasionally families could be seen camping near the river as a rest spot until they moved on. There were a half dozen of this group whose attention was now solely fixed on her. Evidently they had spent the night here and were in no hurry to move along. She simply wished to clean her family's clothing and quickly return to her home. It was still so early in the morning that dawn had not quite made its appearance. She and her husband had departed the hut simultaneously in opposite directions. Though none of the other women had come down just yet, she decided that this was her home and she refused to be intimidated. She smiled and called out to them.

"Good morning, travelers. Welcome to the home of the river people." As she deftly stepped onto the path descending to the river, she felt a slight wind indicating movement at her back. Lilith had never been a coward and she was not about to become one at this stage of her life. When she turned to confront whoever was behind her, a large muscularly built young man stood in her path. Since she was an extremely tall person, she was staring him straight in the eye. He wore a leering smirk on his face.

"Is there a problem, young man?"

Standing as tall as she could, her spine was straight and her shoulders square. From this perspective, she saw that the youth leaning toward her was almost as young as her boys.

"If you were my woman, I would not have allowed you out of my bed so early this morning."

"Since I am not 'your woman', it is a meaningless point."

She thought that others should begin to come soon and she was not going to give him the satisfaction of thinking that she was afraid. Unfortunately, she did not have her staff this morning. Who would have thought of encountering danger so close to home in this situation?

"Perhaps, you should return to wherever your woman is."

A ripple of guffaws passed from one of his friends to the other as they playfully nudged one another with elbows. He knew that his manly image was at risk.

"Ah, you are spirited, as well as beautiful. I believe that you might need a man such as I am, young, strong and willing."

"I have a man. And this is a pointless conversation."

She turned to continue on her way, feeling that this boy was no real threat. As she turned, the young stranger reached out and put his hand on her shoulder. One of his friends moved in closer. Before Lilith had an opportunity to brush his hand away, a blur came hurtling through the air. Her son had appeared out of nowhere, tackling the larger man to the ground. In a heartbeat a frenzied struggle occurred, leaving the man ominously still. In a continuous arc of motion, Asmodo lashed out at the closest of the stranger's companions. Another violent thrashing ensued, within a few seconds a horrible scream tore from the stranger's throat. By this time the others had scattered. The boy had attacked like some demon from hell, leaving two men dead in the blink of an eye. People from the village had begun to gather, standing about muttering and shaking their heads in disbelief. Lilith was in shock, her body shaking unceasingly. Asmodo had come and put his arms about her. For the first time she realized that he was now as tall as she at barely thirteen summers old. What had happened? Where had her baby gone? This tall young man had taken her child's place. How had he managed to kill two men in such a manner? He had not hesitated. But she was not even sure where he had come from. Or how he had known that she was in danger? Adaama arrived in a trot, pushing his way through the crowd. He had still been within noise range and had heard the screams. He gathered his wife and son into the shelter of his arms. What in the name of the gods had happened here? The questions ran through his mind. He was thankful that neither of them had come to harm. Some of the men from the village removed the bodies of the dead men to be buried in a common grave if unclaimed by the day's end. Since they were strangers to the region, it was unlikely that they would escape this fate. The family went to the confines of their home where Adaama insisted that Lilith lie down. When she fell asleep, he spoke quietly to his son.

"What happened out there? Who were those men? How did you happen to come to your mother's aid? "

Unlike his mother, the young man was not at all agitated, or excited. He calmly explained to his father that he, too, had headed out to hunt that morning. Movement had caught his eye when he looked toward the river. He had quickly spotted his mother and rushed to her assistance. His father carefully chose the next question.

"Son, was it necessary to kill them both?" Adaama kept his eye on the way his son reacted.

"I did it. Have you forgotten that there were many of them? I needed to stop it all. There was not a question about killing him. He should never have put his hand on her."

The boy might well have been discussing killing game, or tilling the soil for that matter. Never had the man seen such detached discussion of death. Even though men were sometimes called upon to kill in self defense such a callous attitude was rare.

"But son, you were perfectly capable of stopping the man, even disabling him. Taking the life of another human is a serious issue. Did you think to simply stop him by wounding him?"

"He put his hands upon my mother. Even if you do not value her appropriately, I do." His reply was arrogant and disdainful.

Adaama was shocked by his reply. He raised his voice angrily.

"Why would you say such a thing? There is no question of my disrespecting your mother. I am simply saying that you could have stopped him without murdering him!"

The boy remained calm. He looked at his father this time without any expression. His handsome face betrayed nothing when he turned and walked from the dwelling. Adaama collapsed into a heap on the floor. He buried his head in his arms. What manner of man had they created? What must be going through his poor mother's mind?

Lilith slept through the middle of the day. When she finally awakened, the morning's events came tumbling back into focus. A chill went through her, remembering that two men had died at the hand of her son. She was not convinced that the stranger had constituted a real threat, or just a nuisance. The level of fear had not been that great, at least now she did not think so. Had she seemed afraid? Perhaps that was the problem. She had given signs that she was afraid and Asmodo had reacted to that. Reviewing things over and over, it continued to present the same picture. Her son had over reacted. The deaths of the two young men could not be excused easily.

Asmodo began to spend more and more of his time away from his parents' dwelling. Oddly, it seemed to be the best solution despite his youth. While neither of them discussed it with the other, his presence made them uneasy. No one was quite sure where he spent all of his time, but it was rumored that he and several other young people had moved in with a very young widow in the next village. She had once been a second wife, but her old husband had died, the devoted first wife shortly after, leaving this young childless woman with all of their worldly goods. The former child bride was attempting to recapture her youth. Only his grandfather questioned Asmodo's absence. Happily, the youngest son busied himself with growing up to be a man. He spent his days tilling the fields and had begun to demonstrate exceptional skills at carving. Many of his evenings were spent at the fire of the old carver. Several of the more talented youngsters had almost moved into the large hut. Lilith and Adaama were alone too much of the time. They began to fall into the old patterns of behavior.

18

NAIIMI'S OLDEST DAUGHTER had come of age and would be presented in the next coming of age ceremonies. Her shy, sweetly, sensitive temperament made her reluctant to consider leaving her mother's home. She was as petite as her mother, but prettier. The golden brown tones of her skin were unusually appealing. Across the bridge of her nose was a fine sprinkling of tiny brown spots. Coupled with the dimples in her cheeks, this contributed to her extremely pleasant appearance. A wealthy young man from a neighboring province had laid eyes on her at a summer festival. He had returned home and convinced his family that he had met the girl of his dreams. His doting father and mother had promptly come with him to visit the village. To the astonishment of the local citizens, they proceeded to pay court upon the entire family in a royal fashion. It appeared evident to most that the boy was smitten with the girl because she looked a great deal like his mother. His mother, in turn, loved the girl immediately because she bore the resemblance. She had never had a daughter and could not have chosen a better match for her son. Since he was a handsome, well-bred young man who was head over heels in love with her, the girl found him irresistible. After much consideration and thought, Naiimi was satisfied that he was what he seemed to be. Most importantly, she did not detect any of the telltale signs of a future wife beater. Besides his mother was a formidable woman who would brook no such behavior. The decision was made to allow certain departures from the village traditions.

The wedding was to be held in the groom's village at the second new moon. Much planning and preparation had gone into the occasion. Naiimi had spent long hours in the design and weaving of the exquisite fabric for her daughter's wedding gown. She felt that she had truly created her masterpiece. The loosely woven fabric had repeated the pattern in the same pale yellow color. Her shawl covering her head was exactly the same color and pattern, but was sheer because she had lessened the lines of thread. For some time she had been eager to experiment. It was only fitting that this was her best work. She loved her daughter and wanted to make this wedding special for her. When the marriage had been announced, the headman had come to Naiimi and presented a small package to her.

"I think that it might be the right time to consider giving this to our bride." He said as he helped her to open it.

In her hand was jewelry so delicately carved that it resembled lace. Upon hearing of the wedding, the headman had presented her with these items saved from the package returned to the village so long ago. A bracelet and matching necklace were carved with fine trace work that further highlighted the ancient patterns. The earrings, which were also enclosed, were the final touch to complete the gift. The exquisite beauty and delicacy suited her daughter. She then realized that this was part of Bhutu's ivory. He had done good work. Maybe that had been part of his problem. His artistic frustrations had overwhelmed him. This was a wonderful thing for their daughter, a final good memory of her father to take with her. It was a fitting addition to her dowry. It had not been a simple road to walk in life, raising the girls alone. But now it was almost done. The girl was going to be a truly beautiful bride embarking upon a grand life.

Lilith and Adaama were a part of the large contingent traveling to the wedding. The family of the groom was sparing no expense. Nothing like this wedding had ever been seen in the entire area. For this reason the villagers went to great expense in order to present themselves appropriately. Wonderful garments had been created to clothe them all in a royal manner. Lilith was to wear robes of saffron and gold. Shoes had even been created to match her clothing. She was anticipating the event in much the same manner that she had looked forward to at the time of her own wedding. Her outward appearance had changed little since that time. There was no question that she had retained her carriage, shapeliness, the silky texture of her skin and her grace. Her thick, kinky hair was as long and lustrous as it had ever been. When she wove it up into the braids favored by her people, it was difficult to tell that she was the mother of two almost grown sons. Too often, she was subject to the unwanted attentions of men because of the way that she looked. Her regal carriage and conduct generally removed any actual threat to her person.

A goldsmith in the next village had crafted a set of jewelry to accent Lilith's wedding attire. Not only had he created earrings, rings, a necklace and bracelets, but a set of finely turned gold wires would adorn her upper arms as well. He had offered his services to her at minimal cost, hoping that others of influence would see his work and seek out his services. It was an ingenious idea, so much so that both she and her mother would be wearing his work. The men had laughed at the vanity of the women. However, they did not reject the fine garments constructed for their own use. In all, the river people would be representing this bride from their village in the most splendid manner that they could possibly manage.

The groom and his family lived near the edge of the great desert. The home was built in the manner of those in the eastern city. It was large, airy and its many rooms were constructed from earthen materials. When the guests arrived, each family was shown to private rooms set aside for their use during the festivities. While those guests close to the family were housed in the home, others were made comfortable in a large temporary campsite, adjoining it. Servants had been engaged to meet the needs of the guests by day and night. Even though the river people lived comfortably, none of them were accustomed to such luxury. When they gathered for the evening meal after their arrival, the conversation was animated and full of anecdotes about the things they had seen.

Lilith spent most of her time with the Naiimi and the bride. A full suite of rooms had been provided for their use. Surrounded by the giggles of the two daughters, the older women felt just as silly. They went from room to room examining the quarters that were going to be the bride's new home. Evidently his parents had built these rooms for the couple with every luxury possible. Anyone nearby would have heard the gales of laughter coming from the rooms on the evening before the wedding. The four women pampered themselves with beauty potions, creams and lotions. Each intended to look her absolute best on this auspicious occasion.

Adaama had spent some time with the headman after the meal. Afterward he walked alone past the courtyard. It was easiest that he see that their animals were fed, and find any other tasks to occupy himself. He was pleased that the girl was marrying well. It was hard to believe that so much time had passed. Thoughts of his old friend had crossed his mind recently. Bhutu would have been very proud that his lovely daughter was marrying so well. In fact, he would have been beside himself. After all, the truth was that he had been a bit of a braggart. That his daughter had married into such a family would have had the little fellow walking on clouds.

Adaama chuckled to himself and gathered the feed to take out. He bumped into a stable hand, who was himself feeding animals. As he caught sight of Adaama, he could not understand why any of the guests would want to muck the animals. But it meant less work for him, so he ignored the man. When he completed the task that he had assigned himself, the tall blonde river man started back to the rooms. He knew that with the ways of women and weddings, Lilith would not likely return soon. As he passed the campsite, someone called his name.

"Ho, Adaama! That is you!" A cousin approached and grasped his hand heartily.

"Well, hello my kinsman. I had not known that I would see any of my family here."

"Yes, several of us arrived within the hour. Others who live near-by are coming in the morning. The groom's family has done business with many of our family over the years."

The two kinsman exchanged pleasantries for a while longer. The encounter was a surprise to each of them. Since the two were of like age and station, each was extremely glad to meet his cousin. Like most married men, neither had looked forward to a wedding with the same enthusiasm as the wives had. They decided to share the morning meal and parted ways after appointing a time to meet.

When Adaama entered the house, his spirits were much higher. This visit was not going to be as much of a social chore as it had started out being. His step was lighter and he hurried toward the southerly wing in which he was housed. As he turned into the hallway, a door in to one of the rooms ahead of him opened. Standing in his path was the pale dancer from years before. Because it was indoors, his fair young kinswoman was without any scarves or head coverings. The shock of seeing her was even more vivid than the last time. Her golden hair shimmered in the flickering lamplight. It was again braided and the braids were adorned with blue colored stones. Her ears, neck and arms were laden with pieces crafted with the same stones. She wore a robe of the same azure shade, which was reflected in her pale eyes. His thought was that her eyes were the sea and he would drown. As he was entranced, she was equally. She had managed a long glimpse of this tall man at the campsite. Her first thought had been that he looked strange. But it dawned upon her that they were alike, and he was actually pleasing to behold. He stood a full head taller than she, with broad shoulders and sturdy, well formed legs. Unlike hers, his skin was slightly burnished by the sun. Peeking from beneath his head covering, his hair was the golden color of the morning sun. The eyes that stared back at her were the deep dark blue of a summer sky. They sat on each side of a finely drawn nose. His jaw was noble and showed strength. He was, indeed, a handsome man. Without a word passing between them, they each knew. Some recognition passed between their souls. They stood transfixed, unable to either move forward or retreat. Finally he was rendered capable of speech. His voice was thick and raspy, as though his throat was parched.

"You are Eve."

She raised her face, fully exposing the lovely lines of her neck. The web of blue stones in her necklace sparkled like stars at twilight. Her voice was as melodic as the tinkling of bells, "And you, are my kinsman Adaama."

"Not close kin." He felt it necessary to establish this. Her grand-father was a cousin to his grandmother. The degree of sanguinity was negligible at this point. They were only, loosely, members of the same family tree.

When she smiled, it was the answer to his every question. "No, not close kin."

The issue was raised and put away. He knew then that in these few words, his world changed. He could only go forward from this point.

"Are you traveling with your parents?"

"No, I have no one close since my grandparents died. I am sharing the room with a kinswoman. We were given the room because we are young women alone."

"And where is she?" Adaama was uncharacteristically bold. He needed to know everything that he could about her.

"Why sir, is that of interest to you? "Her tone was lilting, teasing.

He began to turn away. Reason began to seep into his brain. The girl wanted to play with him. She was very much the vixen, aware of his desire for her. What could he be thinking? At that moment, she put her hand on his upper arm. The touch was electric. Her tone had changed completely.

"She will return shortly, perhaps we can speak tomorrow."

He turned to look at her one last time. In that single glance it was assured that they would indeed speak tomorrow.

She retreated to the inside of the room. He briskly walked to his own quarters. As he approached the room, he suddenly realized that he prayed to be alone now. Hopefully, Lilith would be busying herself with the wedding preparations. He needed his wife to be absent from him, as it was now clear that he could no longer deny his heart. Luckily, she had not returned. After a short period of restless anxiety, he fell promptly asleep, dreaming of azure eyes.

When Lilith returned, she was exhausted. She did not stir until shortly after the dawn and performed her morning ablutions. She was already in the midst of dressing her hair when Adaama awakened. He lay quietly, feigning sleep until she was fully dressed. She came to the bed and kissed his forehead.

"I will see you at the ceremony", she indicated, then left the room.

"Mmmm," he mumbled and pretended to stir slightly. Never before had it been within him to deceive her. An irrevocable step had been made, if only in his heart to date. He lay motionless for some-time. At full light he rose and poured water into the basin from the large jug. After washing up, he found himself dressing with ceremony. He took extreme care with every aspect of his morning toilette, slowly anointing his body with the oils that he usually ignored. Seldom in his life had he been a genuinely sensual being. Lilith had found him to be an indomitable task over the years. When she had found the patience and the keys, he had discovered that side of himself from time to time. Remarkably, today, he was a new being. It was as though he was newly awakened from a slumber of the senses. He spent time stroking the balsam oils into his face, hair and beard. His hair shone with the glory of the new day. All of the energy spent planning the new clothing for the wedding had seemed frivolous. Now, he lovingly clothed himself in the lavish creamy robes and matching head covering. The smaller rectangle of fabric had truly appeared silly when Lilith had fitted it to his head. It barely sheltered one from the sun. When coupled with the gold circlet of a headpiece, it did look regal. His short robe was cut in a manner flattering to his masculine body. A gold cuff encircled his wrist. Once he was completely clad, he inspected his image in the surface of the bowl of water. As he went to meet his cousin for the morning meal, he paused to take a deep breath. He was ready to face it all.

By the time that Adaama joined up with his cousin, others had also come. The men spent a jovial time recounting the gathering at the summer campsite. He was completely comfortable with this group of his kinsman. Though none were as pale as he, his color did not give them pause. Throughout their clan, the wide variations in complexion had existed for generations. The young men that sat at the table were every beautiful shade that the gods had created, from burnished ebony to Adaama's sun kissed cream. Their ages ranged from early twenties to early thirties. They were a gathering of men in the full bloom of manhood.

When the three young women entered the eating tent, the easy male jocularity stopped as if lightning had struck. Intakes of breath were heard around the table. Each of the girls was a beauty in her own right. Leading them was a darkly olive complexioned girl of buxom proportion. She was clad in green filmy fabric that served to emphasize her ripe qualities. Her full lips looked like a juicy slice of red fruit, waiting to be devoured. In her dark eyes, one could glimpse the warmth of the desert nights. In her wake, followed a frail dreamy looking girl with golden brown skin and high cheekbones. Like Naiimi's daughter, she had the faintest dusting of freckles across the bridge of her nose. Her hair was a slightly deeper shade of brown than she. The red of her robes was matched by the crimson of her mouth. Eve was the third girl. Today she wore an even more

spectacular azure gown highlighted in gold. The blue stones twinkled from her ears, throat, arms and hair. Her willowy presence filled Adaama's field of vision. The most discreet of nods was exchanged. Though each of them was known to someone at the table, none of the men knew them all. Most of the men were married, but this did not lessen the effect. It was as if they had been attacked physically. Shamefully, none of them wished to acknowledge the attack.

After an awkward moment, one of the younger cousins stood and bowed to the trio. Like the clear victors in an undeclared war, they chose to ignore him and moved forward to an empty table. A nervous chuckle made it's way about the table until it became a full-throated laugh. The conversation was resumed only then. At the same time, the wife and toddler belonging to one of the kinsman came to claim him.

Adaama's mind was consumed with speaking to the girl again. His simple need was to be in her presence, alone, or so he told himself. As the group of men broke up, he saw her depart in the direction of the house. He looked about him to be sure that no one from his village seemed to be observing him. A frenetic level of activity was taking place all around the house and grounds. Though a lot of people were moving about, they were all intent upon their own tasks and concerns. He moved quickly through the house to the wing where he had seen her last night. When he reached the door, it opened just as he raised his hand. She pulled him in quickly, pushing him against the heavy rough wood of the door. At the same time she pressed her palms closely to his chest.

"I knew that you would come. Why do *you* think you are here?"

At the same time that she was so close to his body, she held herself separate. Nothing was as important to him at that moment, as dissolving the minute space between them.

"You know why I am here," Adaama put his powerful arms around her slim waist. He lowered his head into the soft, sweet curve of her neck. A wave of heat started at the soles of his feet and encompassed the both of them. The girl felt herself succumb to the cloud of passion engulfing her. It was more real than anything she had experienced in her short life. This beautiful golden man was not a boy to be casually toyed with. While her body had not yet known a man sexually, her soul knew this man to be the mate that it sought. His mouth experienced the taste of her flesh and ravenously sought her lips. Here the subtle difference in the texture drove him wild. He felt that he would devour her. She answered his kisses hungrily. She was totally out of her depth and experience. Nothing in her seventeen summers had prepared her for this assault upon her senses. As quickly as he had begun kissing her, he stopped and pushed her away. Her head swam dizzily. What was happening here? She moved toward him, eager to resume.

Breathing heavily, rapidly, he grasped her forearms and pushed her to arm's length. Obviously, this could not happen here and now. She must have no real idea, he thought and knew that he needed to think. Flushed and panting in a shallow fashion, she stood looking down at the floor. One of her myriad braids had unraveled and hung loosely into her eyes. Her legs were weak.

He adjusted himself and straightened his robe. "Not like this, anyone might come. Tonight during the feasting, meet me near the stables. No one should be there. We must be alone, and we need to talk. I am sorry."

When her ability to breathe returned, so did her ability to speak, to think. Her voice was barely audible when she spoke.

"I am not sure what came over me. We...I..." she attempted to regain her composure. Suddenly she felt like a wanton child. Never had she acted in such a manner. She had been on her own since her grandparents had died. Numerous men had made advances toward her, but she had managed to tease and control them. This man had to be the person meant for her.

"I will be there." She turned to repair her intricate hairdressing and smooth her robe.

He left the room after looking in every direction. Walking rapidly, he approached the courtyard. A bit of fresh air had gone a long way to help him calm his state of mind. The crowd had begun to gather for the wedding. He could see his wife standing at the front of the crowd. Naiimi was nearby. The bridal party was already in place. He noticed the uncanny resemblance between the groom's mother and the bride. Bhutu briefly crossed his thoughts once again. The exquisite ivory jewelry was serving a purpose today. It was a fitting remembrance that the man had at least loved his daughter. Adaama thought that at this moment he was glad that he and Lilith had no daughters, no young children now. Looking at her from across the crowd, he observed that she looked majestic today. He thought that he would like to remember her that way.

Lilith was totally involved, emotionally and logistically, in the events of the wedding. She was happy for the bride, the groom and his family. This was the best day that her friend had experienced in a long while. The groom's mother had asked that Naiimi's younger girl spend at least half of her time with them to avoid the bride's suffering from homesickness. Both girls were excited about life in this new place. Of course this would increase the possibility that the second girl might also find a mate nearby. It was already whispered that the groom's older brother was staking his claim on this younger sister. The solution was a good one for all involved.

Sons were a source of joy, but Lilith unexpectedly felt sorrow because she had never had a daughter. Nothing could explain this abrupt sadness. She looked around the room for her husband. Her parents were situated midway the crowd with some others from their village. It was always a joy to view them from afar. They were such a regal pair. Hana had become even prettier as a mature woman than the callow girl brought back to the village by the young headman. She complemented her handsome husband as they bent their heads together, sharing an intimate moment. Lilith cherished their example. With them around, who could doubt the value of such a union? Finally her eyes located Adaama. He stood at the rear edge of the crowd. At least, he stood near a kinsman. They seemed to be in a conversation. She always worried about his solitary state. It was a good thing that he had located that companion. She turned back to the beginning of the ceremony.

Also scanning the crowd from a less obvious perspective, Eve found his wife, whose face was well known to her. As in any family, information was easily collected. She knew that they had two sons, but neither was a babe in arms. So much information was available about her rival that she was almost infamous. Everyone had heard about her travels and the many rumors. His mother never stopped talking to all who would listen about how much she loved the woman and how close the two families had always been. And yes, Eve had to admit that she was beautiful. Her clothing was especially fetching in the rich saffron and gold colors that flattered the reddish brown tones of her smooth skin. Her body was beautifully formed even now. In any other circumstance, Eve thought that she would admire this woman. But this could have nothing to do with what was occurring between she and the tall man. The girl recognized him as her destiny. He affected her in some way that she could never have imagined. She felt giddy, yet crafty and calculating. She felt so much older than seventeen.

Ravishing was the only description for the bride. Her mother had hoped that the fabric would be beautiful beyond imagination, and this desire had come to fruition. Not only did it serve to create the perfect wedding dress, but numerous requests for similar fabric were being made of Naiimi. Her craftsmanship and artistry had been recognized beyond her dreams. The ivory jewelry that her daughter wore had indeed been the perfect accessory. It turned out that the headman had also kept intact a number of pieces for the younger girl. He had been both entranced with the intricate quality of the work and hoped that Bhutu would have wanted it so. The groom's parents were so proud that incidental acquaintances kept presuming that they were the bride's parents, instead of the groom's, especially since they were busily catering to both girls. Naiimi could not believe how blessed she was. Her daughters had the beginnings for better lives than hers had been. She had suffered after her mother had died. Lilith had been her only solace. These girls would not be so alone.

Piled high in wonderfully elaborate dishes, food of every description was provided for the wedding feast. Sweets, breads, fruits and meats overflowed the tables along with wines brought in from lands far away. The joy of the occasion was certainly carried forward into the feast. Musicians played while dancers danced, creating a raucous party atmosphere that blanketed the house and grounds. It was a blessing that the house stood alone on the edge of the desert since the noise could be heard for miles. Lilith was convinced that this was the best feast she had ever attended.

The massive degree of total pandemonium simplified Adaama's task. He had never reached his wife's side during the ceremony and had easily slipped from the area. It was only required that he plaster a huge smile on his face, hold a drinking bowl in his hand and keep moving. As he walked past the stable, it was certain that even the stable hand must be celebrating tonight. He waited patiently. Nothing stirred in the stalls. It was quiet here at least. Just when he had begun to doubt that she would come, she appeared out of the shadows. The blue of her robe was bleached white in the moonlight. Light reflected from the many stones she wore, giving her an ethereal look. Her graceful sway made her seem to drift...like some ghostly apparition. He thought to himself that it was odd that someone so alive, so passionate, should convey that nebulous quality. He stepped into her path and took her hands. The look on her face told him everything he needed to know. If he had questions about this, they were instantly silenced. In her eyes he saw himself reflected as he wished. There were no doubts in her eyes. Adaama led her into a secluded section of the stable. It was a freshly built area, still clean and untouched. The fresh sweet smell of the hay was a heady perfume. He folded her into the circle of his arms. She trembled as he kissed her eyes, her face, the tip of her nose. His hands moved over her body with a strength and delicacy that she had only imagined before. Sliding underneath her robe, his fingers took on a life of their own. Fingertips glided to touch her breasts with the faintest of pressure. The circular motion lit a white-hot flame that began to spread slowly across the surface of her skin. No one could have described the depth of this feeling to her. When he moved his mouth to replace his fingers, her breathing stopped. His hands had trailed down the length of her body, lingering to stroke and caress. She was rendered incapable of independent movement. Her body had become a reactive thing, responding to his touch. Instinctively, she was unafraid even though this was all new. Without a doubt, she was made for the pleasure that this man was generating in her body. Why had no one told her that such exquisite sensation was possible? He began to stroke her thighs softly. The lingering caresses suddenly took on an urgency. When he reached her center, she began to match the rhythm of his movement. Her body had become a separate wanton, uncontrolled being. As he quickly removed her robe, he gazed at the rosy tips of her breasts. The color was as flushed as if reflecting a flame. There was indeed a fire, which had begun to erupt between the pale columns of her thighs. He slipped out of his own robes in a single swift motion and proceeded to kiss the entire pale sweetness of her. Eve, captive to the wanton who controlled her, lay trembling, waiting for whatever pleasure he chose to gift upon her body. When his mouth glanced the skin of her thigh, the trembling became a spasm. He proceeded to render the sweetest of kisses to the very core of her being. Her body became a raging thing in constant spasm. Her legs repeatedly shook. By the time that he slipped between her knees, she eagerly sought what ever came next. He had never felt so in control of his sexuality. Now, he had found the partner that he could lead in the dance. The rhythm was perfect.

The lovers lay spent in the moonlight. Reality began racing into Adaama's head and he saw that he had opened a door from which he could not return. As he ran his fingers through the wheat colored braids, he knew that his future lay with this girl, this woman. They had barely exchanged a dozen words, but their souls had better knowledge of one another than anyone he had known in life. She had no close family left, but him. Adaama understood that he was her family now. His first thought was that he could marry her and continue his life in the same way. It was possible. Others took second wives. He then knew that he could not do what others did.

"Are you all right?" He asked. When she smiled, it was clear that her body was as sated as his. "I am sorry if I hurt you."

She started to laugh. It was a low throaty sound.

"I have been waiting for you. I did not know it before. But I have been waiting for you. I have dreamed of a special man. When my kinswomen had spoken of men, it never seemed real. Because I am different perhaps..." Her voice trailed off.

"You are beautiful. I too have been waiting for you. Do you trust me?" He held her shoulders and looked into the depths of her eyes.

"Of course. You are everything to me." The innocent sincerity of her youth was overwhelming.

He could not resist smiling. "You don't know me, but thank you for believing in me." It was strange, but they were completely in the same vein of thought.

"My Adaama, I do know you. Now in every way possible, I know you. I trust you and we should both be going back now. Someone is sure to miss one of us."

Eve tidied herself with straw. A few twists and pins put her hair in order. When she pulled her robe back in place, she only looked more beautiful, flushed with a bloom that had risen to her entire upper body area. He took her face in his hands and hungrily covered it in kisses.

"How long had you planned to be here?" He had to determine a plan of action.

"I don't live very far from here. Didn't you know that? Or was I the only one who was curious? "

"What do you mean, curious?" He had no idea what she referred to. When she explained that she had also seen him at the campsite gathering that summer, he was shocked. She was a constant source of surprise and joy.

"I saw you when I was dancing. After I recovered from the shock, I thought that you were the most beautiful man that I had ever seen. I closed my eyes and danced for you. Since then you have inhabited my dreams. I knew that we would meet again."

The look on her face was both innocent and cunning. She had claimed him on that day so long ago, dancing for him alone. They parted separately, agreeing to meet on the next evening. Upon rounding the tents he bumped into two of the cousins with whom he had broken the morning's bread. Adaama thought for moment that he saw an odd expression pass between them. His normal instincts were somewhat dulled and he dismissed his concern. After exchanging overly hearty greetings, he went on his way.

Lilith's eyes had not rested for the whole evening. Despite the lovely affair, she was no longer having a pleasant time. Hours ago, she had realized that her husband was nowhere to be seen. She said nothing to anyone, but her level of upset had reached the sky by now. It was impossible for her to leave the festivities, so she suffered silently. When he did finally appear, she knew that something was awry. Even without smiling, he wore an almost jaunty expression. Initially, she thought that it had to do with his kinsmen being present. He was so often so solitary. It had been a refreshing sight earlier. At that moment, Lilith caught a disturbing glimpse in of the corner of her eye, a young woman done up almost as fetchingly as the bride with braids intricately done and unique jewelry of blue stones sparkling from her person. It had been, what four or five summers ago? Even so, there was no question that it was the girl. She looked directly at her and knew where her husband had been. Eve gazed boldly into her eyes. Her azure stare was mocking and confident. Lilith turned back to look at Adaama. The exchange had not escaped him. Somehow it no longer mattered. For different reasons, Lilith also decided that it no longer had significance. Along came a charming foreign man who had earlier spoken to her. She engaged him in conversation this time. At this moment, she needed to feel desirable.

The rest of the evening was spent in an odd social state. Many of the river people had noticed Lilith's behavior by now. Her parents were each attempting to unravel the puzzle without bringing any more attention to the situation. Their daughter was shamelessly flirting with several men. Even as a girl, she had never been a flirt. Indeed, she and Naiimi were the center of attention. She was virtually holding court in the center of the room. When the headman looked about for Adaama, he was unable to locate him. Creating a spectacle was not her way. Her father could not decipher the course of events that could have caused his daughter to act this way.

Lilith returned to her quarters late at night. Adaama was nowhere to be seen. "Could he be with her?" She dismissed the thought. Adaama was not that kind of man. Perhaps he was enjoying the revelries. Actually, her husband had fled to the stables with a wineskin and fallen asleep alone in the hay. About dawn, Lilith was awakened as he stumbled back to the room. The aroma of the wineskin emanated from his pores, bits of straw clung to his clothing. She lay there fully conscious, not wishing to confront him. Even though she was certain that he had had some contact with the girl earlier, the words had not passed between them. He fell asleep quickly, not wishing to have to speak to his wife.

Around daylight, Lilith awakened, washed and dressed. She sat quietly in the window combing the fluffy swath of long hair that lay about her shoulders. In her hands was an ivory comb that her father had given her after her womanhood ceremony. The ivory had mellowed into a shade of soft cream. She realized that almost twenty summers had passed since that event. The months that she had suffered waiting for her life to begin, came tumbling back into her mind. If her father had not approached Adaama, would he ever have declared his interest? She could not help but wonder, especially in light of the present state of affairs. Had he ever really wanted her? It had taken such long time for them to achieve real intimacy. He had been reluctant and skittish. She, on the other hand, had been seething with desire. Maybe because she had always kept herself wound so tightly, she had let herself relax when she married the man that she loved. All these years were wasted. She was absolutely certain of some kind of involvement with the girl. The look on that brazen little vixen's face was not mistakable. Should she wake him and make him admit it?

When she completed the dressing of her hair, she decided to go to the morning meal. She was not going to stoop to that level.

When Lilith entered the tent, she could have sworn that the buzzing of conversation had actually paused. After collecting her food, she sat with some other women. She sensed that her imagination had not been overactive, there was some attention directed toward her. One of Adaama's kinsmen was staring openly at her. There was an oddly inquisitive expression on his face. She could not determine if his stare was positive or negative. Once she had eaten, Lilith felt refreshed, ready to stand up to the day. While walking out of the enclosure, Lilith paused and greeted the young man who had been guilty of staring at her. His reaction was flustered and embarrassed when she spoke to him and inquired after his well-being.

Her mother and father were in the open courtyard as she neared the house. They had arisen early and had eaten their morning meal. As Lilith walked up to her mother and embraced her, Hana examined her daughter closely. She remained completely confused by her daughter's actions of the prior evening. When they had retired, Lilith was still at the festivities. It did not seem that she was worse for the wear this morning.

"Did you enjoy the evening's events?"

"Yes, Mother. There were many interesting people. Of course, I was so happy about the wedding. Was the bride not lovely?" Lilith's chatter was bright, a little too brightly done for her mother's taste.

Hana reminded herself that her daughter was no longer her baby girl. "Yes, and it has been a wonderful time. However, we must return to our regular lives. Are we still departing at the next dawn?"

Lilith deferred to her father, "Baba, Is that correct?"

The headman could not understand why the women were chatting mindlessly. The plan had not been changed. At times it seemed that they spoke to assure themselves that they continued to retain the ability to do so.

"Of course, why would it have changed?"

Hana was amused to hear the annoyance in his voice. She knew exactly what thoughts were going through his mind. She sought to change the subject.

"Whatever will Naiimi do without both daughters?"

Lilith promptly expressed her opinion, "She will most likely wear out her arms on the looms. Weaving is her single passion. I believe that it will be for the rest of her life."

Her mother could not help but note her concern. "But she is still a young enough woman. Might she not marry again? Surely now that her daughters are grown up..." Her voice dissolved in confusion.

"No, I believe that her hurt is so deep, she will never let go. She thought that Bhutu was her friend, as well as her husband. He beat her and abandoned her, destroying her trust."

Hana could not understand these younger women. One had to continue to make the effort. "Well, one has to allow healing. You know that."

Lilith could not help but think that her mother's own experience with men was unique and perfect. She could not expect everyone else to feel the same way.

"Mother, you are correct of course. But not everyone is as blessed as you have been as far as men go."

Hana quickly replied, "Or as you are."

When her daughter did not respond promptly, Hana prodded her. "Dear?"

"Oh, yes Mother," her mind no longer was there.

The older couple departed to tour the property with the groom's family. Lilith was left to her own devices. Her own problems were necessarily shoved far back into her mind. She had decided to locate Naiimi and took the path toward that area of the house. Maybe they could view the gardens together. The interior of the house was cool and dark. Even though it was just mid morning, the difference in the temperature varied greatly inside and out. As she casually strolled through the halls, she thought how wonderful it would be to live in such a home always. Her mind wandered to the eastern cities that boasted such homes. Her visits had been brief and so long ago. All of her recent journeys had been so much closer to home. She smiled to herself and thought that maybe she would travel again. Lilith's pleasant sojourn through the cool hallways was rudely interrupted. As she turned a corner, she bumped into two young women rushing along. While she was certain that they were strangers, both stared at her in a most familiar manner. The taller of the two, a frail and freckled brown girl gave her a haughty backward glance. Lilith searched her memory for the girl's face and when she could locate no frame of reference, was puzzled by her behavior.

When she finally arrived at the right wing of the house, her spirits had risen somewhat. Naiimi wore another brightly colored robe of beautifully crafted fabric. A cheerful smile wreathed her face. Lilith could not remember the last time that she had seen her friend in such buoyant spirits.

They took a leisurely walk through the covered gardens. Flowers had been planted in every manner imaginable. Various urns in every type and color contained the most beautiful flowers either of them had ever seen. An amazing array of colors were scattered throughout the gardens! Naiimi could only wish that she might be able to create dyes in such shades! To be sure, she would make the attempts when she returned to her village. There were colors here that she had never seen before. The two women whiled away the better portion of the afternoon enjoying the vast display of horticultural beauty.

Adaama had lain motionlessly. His head throbbed incessantly. As the light began to pour into the window, the pain became more unbearable. Never in his past had he succumbed to the lure of drink. Now, his entire life had spiraled out of his control. As the events of the past evening flooded his thoughts, he became distraught. It had been so clear then. His senses were deluged with the sensory memories of Eve. It occurred to him that every woman was distinctly unique. Even in his limited experience, he suddenly knew that if he made love to a hundred women, no two would be the same. This girl was uniquely right for him. The smell of her, the taste of her, the exquisite feel of her overwhelmed Adaama again. He realized that he needed to regain his balance here and now. A splash of cold water brought him back into this space...a space he was sharing with his wife. The possibility of taking Eve as a Second Wife re-entered his head. This was a coward's way out. He knew that neither of these women would accept the simple solution. At least he was certain that his wife would not. No one in Lilith's family had engaged in a multiple marriage. His options were rapidly disappearing. His life would be hell if he attempted such an arrangement.

After washing and putting on his robe, he gathered his belongings together. He left them stacked neatly in a corner of the room. Walking at a brisk pace, he headed toward the food. He needed some sustenance to put his body back in order. The bout with the wineskin had not had a good long term effect. To be sure he would not choose that solution again. After picking up some bread and fruit, he found a place to sit and eat. Looking up, he saw three of his kinsmen approaching him. Solemn looks were plastered across their faces. He smiled in acknowledgement, but no smiles were returned in greeting. Adaama was surprised and confused. The oldest of the men sat down closest to him, straddling the bench.

"Adaama, we have serious family business to discuss." His tone was brusque.

"Now?" he responded carefully. This did not bode well. Something was obviously wrong, but he had no idea what this was about.

"It would be better if it were less public," the man's face had remained stern.

Adaama quickly shoveled the last of his food into his mouth.

"Then let us find a more private place to discuss this mysterious matter."

The four men walked out of the tent toward the stable area. It was ironic that Adaama flashed a sudden pleasant memory of his assignation. The group paused and the older man kneeled. The others did so in turn.

"There is a problem, my cousin. This family is one of substance and we do not shirk our responsibilities. In reference to our kinswoman, Eve... She has no close family left. It has been said that you and she..." The man paused delicately. "...have been seen together inappropriately."

Adaama could not believe his ears. Did she do this? Who could possibly have known about them?

"What are you saying? I am a man of honor."

A softer look crossed the man's tan face. He stroked his gray streaked beard.

"We are all men of honor here, Adaama. But this woman is our kin. She is young and had not been with any man..."

A rush of color came up from the tall man's neck as the memory of Eve's innocent wantonness filled his senses, flooded his memory. This could not be happening. How dare they question his honor? Could someone have spied upon them? The thought of someone having observed them in the throes of that amazing passion made him sick to his stomach.

"Why are we here?" he regained his composure.

"Are you admitting your involvement with this young woman?" The man leaned forward toward Adaama.

He became angry now. This was a private matter. What business was it of these men? He asked as much.

"Sir, why are you particularly concerned in this matter, if there is a matter to discuss? Did the young woman in question tell you that I...?"

His voice trailed off. It was a difficult situation. He had no intention of dishonoring her. But much needed to be determined.

This time, the man seemed embarrassed. "No, She has no knowledge of this conversation. The two of you were seen coming from the stables last night. There has evidently been some whisper among the women, perhaps she has confided in someone..."

Adaama decided that he now had the advantage, "Do you mean to tell me that this is about the wagging tongues of gossip? You say you come here like a bunch of old women, chasing rumor? I will not discuss any such thing with you. Because you are my kinsmen, I will show you enough respect to walk away quietly." He stood up and did so. His heart was beating wildly in his chest.

It had taken more courage than he had ever needed to face his quarry in the wild. He was not a fearful man, but he had never had to face anything such as this in his life. He looked back at the men who all wore sheepish expressions as they stared at their feet. Even though this was handled for the moment, he knew that more confusion would come.

It was nearly dusk. This was the final night of the celebration. In the morning the bridal couple would emerge for a breakfast, after which, everyone would depart from that event. It was easy to avoid everyone until then. Eve had remained in her quarters all during the day. She was experiencing both physical discomfort and remorse. When she had gone to her room on the previous evening, she thought that she could still feel the weight of Adaama's body. There was a throbbing sensation between her legs, but oddly enough, it was almost pleasurable. There was no real pain. She had been told that there would be pain. Her cousin had married and told her that her first time was horrible. All that she could think was that the silly boy her cousin married had not been Adaama. A slight shiver went through her as she recalled the ways that he had given her pleasure. It had been wonderful, but what had she been thinking? Later that night, she had seen his wife at the wedding feast. Something strange had happened. When Lilith caught her eye, something had passed between them. Why she had stared at the woman like that, Eve didn't know. Then there had been a horrid, catty scene when her cousin had returned to the room. The girl was older than Eve and had looked at her oddly. She told Eve that she knew what she had done.

"My brother saw you tonight. You and the tall man who is pale like you. He saw the two of you sneaking from the stables."

Eve was shocked. She did not recall encountering anyone.

"I don't know what you mean."

"There is no use denying it. "The girl moved close to her. "I can still smell him on you," she said wrinkling up her freckled nose.

Eve was embarrassed and tearful. Her kinswoman told her that she had been stupid, "What guarantee do you have that he will not walk away? How could you allow yourself to be a toy? You have no dowry and now you have no maidenhead. "

"Adaama is not that kind of man," she was suddenly afraid. The other girl looked at Eve as though she were garbage. Her own dowry was considerable. She was twenty years old, the youngest in her family. But her cold beauty did not attract suitors for long. She had enjoyed having Eve around because she was a novelty. Her ivory skin made her an interesting and unique accessory.

"Don't be foolish. What will you do, be a second wife in some meager dwelling along the river? His haughty wife is bound to make your life a living hell."

Eve did not understand why her cousin was deliberately trying to make her miserable. She flung herself on the sleeping couch in tears. When she left the room, Eve heard her speaking to someone else. Eventually, the voices had faded. She had been left alone. Her kinswoman had chosen to room elsewhere, rather than be tainted by whatever was happening.

Nightfall had finally come. Adaama made the decision to try and catch Eve alone inside. Obviously the stables were safe no longer. He observed that almost everyone was at the evening meal. Only a few servants were moving about. He slipped through the exterior hallways. After gathering his own things, he tapped quietly at her door. He had seen her previous companions together near the fountains, so he thought it safe. When she opened the door and saw his handsome face, her heart was healed. She had suffered alone for the whole day. Her cousin's taunting remarks had bitten deeply. Faint bluish crescents were ringed beneath her eyes, while the dear fullness of her lower lip looked bruised and bitten. Relief leapt into her eyes at the sight of his face. Her misery was apparent at a glance. Adaama took Eve in his strong arms seeking to comfort her. She clung to him and a cascade of tears instantly streamed down her face. He had worried at first that seeing him might trouble her.

"Are you all right with all that has happened between us?"

114

"Yes, Adaama. I needed only to see your face. To be assured of all that I knew when I was in your arms."

She poured out the story of the confrontation with her kinswoman and how she had been alone all day. When she calmed down, he told her to gather her things.

"Whatever our fate, it is together. Are you afraid? "His looked deeply into her eyes. "This might not be an easy way that we have chosen."

Her thought was that he had no idea what her life had been like before. Alone since she was young, she had depended upon the good will of her kinsmen. No one had ever mistreated her, but it was not perfect. She wasted no time packing her clothing. He had donned the sturdy light colored skins that he used for traveling and hunting. She promptly completed the task and made it a point to dress in the same manner that he had. She found it oddly satisfying that her clothing was almost twin to his. They were a well-matched pair. Eve would follow his lead in every way. Not a single question was asked. The tall man and his new mate walked away from the house and camp with a shower of moonlight streaming down to light the northerly path. It seemed to kiss the two heads of golden hair, as well as the golden tan of the skins they wore.

19

WHEN LILITH RETURNED to their quarters, she saw that Adaama's things had been removed from the room. She had not seen him but once during the day. On the way to the evening meal, Naiimi had glimpsed him going in the opposite direction. They had laughed about his bout with the wineskin from the previous night. Since the festivities ended after the next morning's meal, she supposed that he had gone ahead and begun packing the animals and his gear. It was probably a good idea that she should do the same. Lilith proceeded to put all of her clothing in the basket used for that purpose. Her mind remained unsettled about the previous evening's several unsettling occurrences. She decided that it was not a good thing to dwell upon them. It was clear that her husband was going through something, but men sometimes did. Her best method of approach was to ignore it. That girl had been extremely brazen. She could imagine that when Adaama had encountered her, that the pale girl had flirted shamelessly with him. This would have accounted for the look she had given Lilith. Women were so terribly transparent. They took such stock in silly victories.

When the dawn arrived, Adaama still had not appeared. By first light, awareness washed over Lilith and she understood that he would not return. The details were not yet apparent, but she knew that she would not ever see her husband again. The tall woman prepared herself to leave this place. She took her basket and walked to the stables, but she was not the woman who had arrived at this event. When Lilith was accosted by Adaama's kinsmen, she did not respond to their queries. Every word that was said went into directly into her memory. On the surface, in the present she could not accept the events that were occurring around her. It seemed that when the family had sought the girl, Eve, she was nowhere to be found. Someone had seen the two of them departing together. His family disavowed any involvement or prior knowledge of the affair. The man who spoke to her assured her that no one would have approved such actions. If the families had been consulted, perhaps the girl could have been taken as a second wife. Certainly, this could have been an amicable settlement for all involved.

The bearded man approached the headman, attempting to explain his desire that the river people understand that none of their kinsmen had meant Lilith to come to any disrespect. They had confronted Adaama to no avail. The family would cast the both of them from their rolls and his parents would immediately move from the village. Lilith stood like an exquisite mahogany statue. She stood, listened and decided finally that they spoke a foreign language. None of what they said made sense anymore. The small contingent from the village made their departure before the morning feast. Hana was afraid for her daughter. Lilith expressed no emotion. In fact, she refused a mount, walking at the forefront of the group the whole first day. She refused any offer of food or drink during the first leg of the journey. Slowly she began to thirst. The headman made a longer rest period to allow her to recuperate from the pace she had forced upon herself during the day. She did not seem to rest and initiated no conversation of any kind. She only responded when someone spoke to her. Naiimi had made the return journey with them. Even she was treated in the same manner. By the time that the wedding guests reached their homes, the wagging tongues had spread the story of Adaama's desertion throughout this village and every village along both branches of the river. Lilith got only as far as the door of her dwelling. She was heard to utter a prolonged bloodcurdling scream. Some saw her turn and run from the village. No one tried to stop her. It was understood that she needed to grieve the loss of the husband she had loved. If nothing else, her people understood her grief.

A short distance from the village stood a circular growth of trees that dated back to the beginning of time. It was said that the ghosts of the original people lived in this dense forest. Other claimed that the souls of the village dead inhabited this dark and dreary spot. Strips of bark hung jaggedly from the trunks of these ancient trees like so many tattered bits of ragged clothing. Moss dripped from the limbs like so much unkempt, kinky hair. When the wind whistled through, some said the voices of the long dead could be heard bemoaning their cursed fate. In this place, Lilith stopped her flight. She had run until her body collapsed in exhaustion. She curled up inside the base of a tree and slept a fitful, dream filled sleep. In the dream her life was its happiest. She was much younger and the boys were still small. Adaama, sun-kissed and handsome, was about, laughing, playing with them. The little family sat on the bluff overlooking the triangle where the two branches of the river came together. This was the same bluff where they had actually gone in the past. It was a beautiful spring morning. The dappled sunshine was gentle and could not harm anyone. Adaama hadn't even needed his head covering and his golden curls were lustrous in the morning light. She looked closely at herself and saw that she was big with child for a third time. Unlike her real experiences, this was an ungainly pregnancy. Her body was bloated and distended. Her nose had spread across her face. The mask of childbearing was painted into her face. Her ankles were swollen so that her lower legs looked to be the size of saplings causing her movements to be awkward and clumsy. Despite the horrible way that she felt that she looked, her husband continually touched her and told her that she was beautiful. Adaama was sweet and solicitous beyond even his usual self. Suddenly the shadow of a single dark cloud floated across the river and covered them. Sharp and penetrating, the first pangs of labor began. Again the experience did not mirror her life experience as long and wrenching pains wracked her body. Lilith heard the screams ring out repeatedly as she lay writhing in agony with sheet after sheet of clenching pain tearing through her like lightning. No one came to help her. Where were her people? Someone should have heard her cries by now. The women should be at the river by now. Her cries rang out continually. Adaama and the boys stood casually by and watched. Finally, a baby girl was violently expelled from her body. At first glance, she appeared lovely and like her father. Pale gold locks of hair curled about the small head. It slowly became apparent that the baby was carved from the hard, creamy ivory used by the men of the village. Lilith could see herself lying there, weak and bleeding. When she tried to put the ivory creature to her bursting brown breasts, the baby smiled, revealing a complete set of pointed ivory cat's teeth. When she looked up at her mother, there were holes in the center of her eyes and the sky was showing through. Lilith was afraid. She looked to her family for aid. They stood smiling, waving at her as though she was at a distance. When she tried to stand, her strength was logically sapped and she collapsed back onto the grass. Her engorged breasts began to spout streams of blood. When she pushed away the cold ivory doll-like baby, it stood up with reticulated limbs and became the girl, Eve. She took Adaama's hand. They walked away, leaving her lying there, bleeding. Her sons both dissolved into thin air. Lilith woke up howling. She screamed and screamed until she had no voice! Once awake she was thankful that only the souls inhabiting the ancient trees had witnessed her pain. When she could cry no more, she slept a long dreamless sleep.

Upon waking she also found that the forest revealed itself to have another face. Hidden among the dreary trees was a body of crystal water. Some trees nearby were laden with fruit. Surrounding the water were trees filled with flowers that grew by attaching themselves to the bark of the trunks. These flowers were the soft pink and purple colors of the early dawn. An odor wafted from them unlike any she had smelled. Even the perfumes from the east were not so sweetly pungent. Upon closer examination, she saw that the body of water was filled with many other flowers and that a myriad of graceful white birds lived there. This serene place became a haven for Lilith. She had fruit and water to sustain her. Things of extreme loveliness soothed her senses. It was a place of healing.

Each subsequent night that Lilith remained in this magical place, dreams of a different kind came to her. Exotic foreign cities came to her in dream sequences.

Every one was presented in intricate detail. Mornings became a delightful review of the previous night's visit. The sensations were so real as to be palpable. Tastes lingered on the palate. Places of interest became a stored part of her memory banks. There was no doubt in her mind that upon visiting these locations, she would be thoroughly familiar with them all. It became clear to her what her path had to be.

A thinner, somewhat fatigued Lilith came walking back into the village at dusk. She had been away for the entire phase of the last moon. Most of her long dark hair was flying about her shoulders in a fluffy cloud. The majority of her braids had long since unraveled. Though clean and smelling sweetly, she was still clad in her rust colored traveling skins, now slightly streaked with grime. Her face was calm. She smiled, spoke and responded. She had purged her demons.

20

H ANA COULD NOT believe her eyes. For all these days, she had worried about her daughter. Her husband had comforted her, telling her that Lilith had needed to heal. He was sure that she would return once this was accomplished. Hana could only identify with her personal pain, the pain of her daughter's absence. She had never understood the manner in which Lilith dealt with things. She contained her emotions, only to let them totally absorb her. Pain should never be dwelt upon. One needed to continually slough it off in order to move forward. Hana hoped that Lilith would one day learn to deal with life in a less obsessive manner. At first she had thought the woman to be an apparition. Hana saw the clothing and the wild mass of hair flying about in the twilight. An ethereal smile was fixed on Lilith's face as she came walking up to the dwelling. Her mother thought that this must surely be the ghost of her beautiful dead daughter. But she spoke aloud to her mother, "Mama, I am here now."

Her voice was clear and strong. Hana ran to embrace this slightly slimmer version of her dearly beloved offspring. She fretted over her and ascertained that Lilith was indeed in good health. The sparse wilderness diet had sloughed pounds from Lilith's already trim body. She bore few streaks of dirt and grime about her body. Portions of her tangled hair still lay in braids, while the rest was flying about. After pouring water into the large bowls, Hana bathed her daughter in much the same way that she had done for her when she was an infant. After anointing her body with precious oils, Lilith allowed her mother to also wash and dress her hair. Without a doubt, this had not occurred since Lilith was a long legged girl child. After parting her hair with the family's very old ivory comb, Hana lovingly massaged the oils into her scalp. For that brief time, the recently abandoned wife was just her mother's child again.

The headman was away from the village. He had assisted Adaama's parents in moving back to their original home village. The embarrassment of their son's behavior was overwhelming for them. They felt that they had to share some degree of responsibility and shame for his actions. Because of Lilith's family position, it was true that many of their neighbors did harbor some resentment toward Adaama's family. Even though the headman had made it a point to assure them that he did not want them driven from their home, they chose to leave. Lilith's younger son assisted his grandparents and promised to visit them.

Asmodo had moved even further from his home. Disturbing rumors were continually being circulated back to the village about his behavior. His affinity toward cruelty and murder had increased. Strangely, members of his family were no longer surprised, or disbelieving, of the rumors.

After leaving her mother, Lilith walked slowly to her own dwelling. It had been impossible for her to face her home after Adaama's desertion. She was certain that she could do so now. As she entered, it became apparent that someone had come and looked after her things in her absence. The home was as neat and tidy as though someone had been present. She then noticed that everything belonging to her husband had been removed. His beautifully carved bows, his skins and robes, his baskets, were all gone. For a brief moment, she thought that maybe he had come to take them away. But she realized that this could not have been possible. Perhaps her son or her father had thought it best to shelter her from this difficult task. In one respect Lilith had looked forward to the removal of any of Adaama's possessions as a ritual form of purging him from her mind and heart. She stood for a moment, thinking that this space was hers alone now. Never in her life had she lived alone. It was true that her people were communal and few people chose to live alone. She thought that she would like to live just for herself right now. It might be pleasant to have to consider no one else's desires but her own.

Naiimi sat in her usual spot the next morning. A symphony of colors was being created as a rainbow of threads was pulled back and forth. When she spied the tall form of her friend, her response was immediate. During the past month, she had uttered prayers to the gods daily. Just keep her dear sister friend safe! Bring her home from the dark! No one could walk in Lilith's path now, but Naiimi had prayed for her. Now she had come home, a slighter woman, but still her regal self. The petite weaver jumped up and down with joy! She had not spoken to anyone else since early the day before and hadn't had any idea that Lilith had come home.

"You came through it. I am so proud of you!"

"Yes. It was not something that I want to speak about, my friend. It was not easy."

Naiimi looked at Lilith and saw that she had achieved some peace of mind. It had come at a high price, but at least it was done.

"Are you sure that it is purged, Lilith? It took me a long while to think through the pain that Bhutu left me with. Even now, my mind still drifts back at times."

Lilith thought for a moment. Very carefully, she articulated her thoughts.

"When Adaama left, it was as though a piece of my heart were ripped from my living breast. I know now that I loved him because I chose to do so long before I understood what love between a man and a woman could be. I saw my mother and father's union as the perfect one. Now I know that theirs would not be the right one for me. What I had with Adaama was only an imitation of what I need. Poor Adaama! I only hope that he has found what he needs with the girl, Eve. He was never truly happy in this life. Naiimi, now I am going out to find my life."

"What do you mean, 'going out to find' life?" Naiimi didn't quite understand her intent.

"There is a world beyond the confines of this village. We have both seen this. I am about to see as much of it as I can. Think of it! Wouldn't you like to see more gardens like we saw at that house? There are seas that stretch further than the eye can see. Villages filled with more people than we can imagine... Some mountains are so high that they blot out the sun. I am going out to see all that I can see. Soon, I will travel."

"How long will you be gone?"

"I don't know. Perhaps for the remainder of my life, until I see it all."

Naiimi thought for a moment, concluding that she too wished to see more. Lilith was right. There was no reason that they could not go to see as much as they could. She told her friend so.

"Lilith, let us go to look for it. Let us look for everything that we can find."

People who saw them that day wanted to know what had given these two women such amusement. The two of them threw back their heads and began to laugh. They laughed and laughed. The wagging tongues had best prepare themselves for a lot of activity.

21

AT DAWN ON a cool morning at the beginning of what is now called the spring season, a small group gathered in the village common area. Several of the men, including Lilith's brother were going to the closest eastern mountain settlement. They would accomplish some trading and return home. Along with them, Lilith and Naiimi were outfitted in their traveling gear. They had been preparing for this journey for a long time. It remained slightly chilly in the mornings, so they were warmly attired. The gear was constructed of the soft skins that the river people produced. Lilith's costume had been cut from the warm rust colored skins, that she had always preferred since the rich tones were the perfect complement to her skin tones. Her pack and leggings had been made from the same colored material with fur and feather accents. She was a picture of majesty in the early morning light. Naiimi's petite frame was also covered head to toe in clothing made of skins. The ochre shade that was used in her clothing was equally flattering to her golden brown skin tones.

The two women were finally beginning the journey that they had looked forward to since the previous summer. It had been a difficult process. Almost everyone that was close to them objected to such travels by two unaccompanied women. Even though Lilith had been on various missions for her people, the headman did not question her need to go out into the world at large. Her mother was totally distraught. Hana reminded Lilith that in much of the foreign world, women without the protection of men were viewed as prostitutes. Why her daughter would put herself in the way of such peril was totally beyond her. She understood that the end of Lilith's marriage had been traumatic to her. She could not comprehend why she did not look to find a new husband. There was a likely widower or two about. After all her daughter was a beautiful woman still. There was even the chance that she could bear more children. None of it made sense. Hana felt that the experiences of both women must have unbalanced them in some way. It made no sense. On the evening before, she had made one last entreaty to the both of them. After sharing the evening meal, they had sat quietly around the fire to ward off the streak of winter's chill that had lingered past its season.

"I suppose that your minds remain set upon leaving?" The fire cast a warm glow upon her face. Even now it was completely unlined. The skin about her jaw was tight and firm. The occasional streak of silver in her hair was complimentary.

Lilith looked at her mother closely, thinking that she was so lovely. "Mama, nothing has changed. We had always planned to go as soon as the snow cleared in the far mountain passes."

Hana turned to Naiimi, "What are you thinking, my weaver friend? Your daughter is giving birth in the early summer. You will miss that. What would your mother have thought?"

The two younger women passed a knowing glance between them. Hana was using all of her strongest weapons. Naiimi smiled sweetly as she replied.

"Mama Hana, my daughter will be in the care of her husband and his family who love her without limit. She will be fine. But who knows what fate will offer, I might possibly be there. At any rate, I will see the baby at some point before it is too grown up. This journey is important to both of us for different reasons. I want to see and experience new things in order to create a new and different direction for my work. The cloth has been my life since Bhutu." She suddenly looked down in silence. Even among these dearest of people, it was difficult to express her feelings.

Lilith thought that her own feelings might be even harder to explain. Her father had always been tolerant of anything she chose to do. Even now, he was her one ally. He sat listening to his wife make this last plea, knowing that he would have to comfort her for a long while this time. It was clear to him that his daughter was looking for those parts of herself that she had ignored. He had never thought that she should be contained within the confines of the small village of the river people. She was an intelligent person with an unusual grasp for the human condition. He knew that his daughter was a special person. His only concern was time. As he treasured the look of her at this moment, he worried that he may never see her again in this life.

Lilith's thoughts virtually mirrored those of her father. "Mama, Baba, it might be a long time before I see you again. This is the one concern that I have, but I must go. I have no worries about my sons. They were my gift to the world. One of them causes sorrow. It's true. But I cannot dwell on this. I only know that my life has been a shadow up to now. I loved a man who did not know how to love me through no fault of his own. It is my right as a human being to try to find some one who can. Perhaps I won't find that. But, most of all, I must learn to love myself. The joy can be found in the journey. I will take that journey. Naiimi is my sister and neither of us found what was right for us. We have each had to bear terrible loss, each having served as witness for the other during these events in our lives. We will witness the search together."

Hana sat there, the tears rolled down her face, pooling in the hands that were loosely clasped in her lap. She was convinced that this was the last time that she would see her beloved daughter's face.

In the morning, no one other than the travelers stood out in the cold. The headman had said his goodbyes on the previous evening. At this moment, he lay with his arms tightly around an inconsolable Hana. But the mood of this group was one of high spirits. Several of these men had made other journeys, but each of them was thrilled to be embarking on a new adventure. The presence of the women created an additional element of stimulation. These two women had always added some level of drama to village life, therefore this journey was likely to be the source of many a story around future fires.

The group ferried the eastern branch of the river and set out on their way. The roads were in good shape at this time of year because rain had not brought any disasters as of yet. From time to time a deluge could wash out certain of the less well-established thoroughfares. This was especially true in the higher elevations near the great gateway. The band of mountains that ran beside the Red Sea allowed a crossing here. This natural opening in the mountains was the beginning to roads that led to other lands. In the past, Lilith had made her journeys to those lands just east, then south beyond the mountains, at the edge of the Red Sea. She had seen many things in her trips to those cities. While this had been quite an exploit, she needed to see more. The kingdoms just beyond the great gateway offered many delights. Lilith intended to see as much of them as possible. She wished to eat the foreign foods, live under foreign roofs, see the stars under foreign skies.

At the pass that led to the mountain settlement, Lilith and Naiimi parted ways with the men. The two siblings shared an emotional goodbye. Lilith's brother was not happy with his sister's choice to go. However he could identify with her feelings. It was not difficult for him to comprehend the pain she suffered when Adaama deserted her. His own family was the most important thing in his life. His son, Obi was almost as tall as he now. The girl was beginning to grow up. At times she reminded him of a young Lilith. Her long legs and coltish beauty were almost identical to that of his sister at that age. He only prayed that her life would be happier than his sister's had been. Lilith had never deserved the things she had been forced to bear. She had been a good wife and mother. Her service to the village had been exemplary. Their father was going to miss her most. As he turned away and raised his hand in farewell, he only hoped that the headman remained healthy enough for her to return. He looked back from time to time. His sister became smaller and smaller as she walked toward the new life. Finally she was gone and he hoped not for the last time. At last sight, he knew that she was becoming larger to the world beyond his.

22

9/7/19
there

THE BEGINNING OF this journey was exhilarating for the
women. Each step brought some new experience. The crisp fresh
air smelled sweeter than any that either of them had inhaled in the
past. A rare pretty little blue blossom grew up high in these mountain
passes. The color was as vivid as Lilith's eyes. They each took turns
picking these blooms. It was as though they were children again with
a new playground. The plants were going to be the base for a new
dye Naiimi assured Lilith. She could not wait to get started once they
were settled someplace for a while. A robe of the same color as her
friend's eyes was an amazing thought. Their concerns were once again
focused upon themselves. They saw few other travelers at this point,
but this put no damper on their spirits. Songs and rhymes helped
the miles pass. It seemed that weaving was not Naiimi's only talent.

As they hiked along the trail, her vocal efforts were of extraordinary quality. Lilith had been known to have a melodious voice, but hers was mediocre compared to that of the tiny weaver. Lilith loved the sound of her friend's voice. She found it difficult to believe that she had been unaware that her friend sang in such a manner. It seemed to Lilith that walking along in this beautiful place while listening to such a voice was a tribute befitting the gods. She wondered why such was not done.

The Great Gateway was finally visible in the distance. Feeder trails had begun to dump travelers into the main road after the women began to descend from the higher road. A few families were seen struggling to keep themselves together. Other assorted groups had matched up on the road and had no difficulty keeping up with one another. A few farmers were seen herding varied fowl and animals to the markets of the city closest to the gateway. A carnival like atmosphere prevailed as they approached the walls of the city.

It was the middle of the day. Naiimi's stomach was filled with butterflies. Here she was at the walls of the great city. Who would have believed that she would end up so far from the village of the river people? She watched Lilith out of the corner of her eye. The tall woman was calm and serene with nothing seeming to ruffle her surface. Well, almost nothing, certainly nothing that was not life altering. Lilith stood in her usual regal glory waiting to enter the city's gates. It was always interesting to see her in the midst of strangers. Not only because of her height did she stand head and shoulders above those around her. Because of her air of presence, she was accorded the deference due a queen. Naaimi saw that her friend was exactly the same person that she had been when they chased through the village as children. Even then people treated Lilith differently because she carried herself like a queen. No one wanted to engage in games in which she didn't play. Lilith's voice snapped her out of her reverie.

"What do you think about? Are you very excited? Here, there is a place that we will go. Once before I came to this city, so I am somewhat acquainted with it. Besides, I am also acquainted with someone who has offered the shelter of his roof to the both of us on our journey."

"What? Who is this person? Did you truly have a lover Lilith? Were the wags correct this time?" Naiimi could not believe her ears.

"Of course not. He is a man who is friend to my father. He is someone that I have known since I was quite young. I have taken no lovers as of yet. But I no longer rule out the possibility. I am a woman without a man. Remember?"

"I know that, however it is something that I have not chosen to venture into in the past. The available fare in our home village helped to curb my appetites. It had not yet occurred to me that this journey would change that." Naiimi shook her head in disbelief.

Lilith could not help but laugh at her friend. At the same time she truly understood why she would think in such a manner. The wagging tongues could curb many an appetite. So much of their lives had been ruled by the wags. It was time to ignore them. She was a woman who had lost her mate. A full-grown woman who had to look after her own needs. She would rule her own life now. No man and no gossips would rule her.

"This journey is about my life as a woman who will no longer subject herself to a man. Too much of my life has been spent worrying about and caring for a man before myself."

"But this is the way it is supposed to be. This is the way we have been taught," said Lilith, even though she agreed with Naiimi in her heart, "Just because something *was*, it does not have to continue to be. Tradition supports itself, Naiimi. When everyone does what they are told...what everyone before them has done, nothing changes. If Adaama had done what he had been told to do, we would all have been miserable. I would NOT have been happy having that girl as a Second Wife." She thought for a brief moment and laughed aloud.

"But thinking of it, I would NEVER have accepted that. I thought that I wanted what my parents have. I might never have been able to determine that I was wrong if he had not run away with his precious little mirror image."

After a few moments, she answered Lilith. "I don't know why I am the one to say anything. I did refuse to take a chance again. If I had married another man who raised his hand to me, I would have killed him. If it meant that I had to wait until he slept, I swear that I would have killed him." A solemn shadow crossed Naiimi's face.

"Well, my friend we are both here on this road because we had the nerve to make choices. Even if we did not cause those events that forced us to make the choices, we made them. Let us cheer for ourselves."

Lilith looked about as they finally passed through the gates to ascertain herself of her bearings.

"We must go in this direction. The dwelling of our host lies there."

They turned in the direction she indicated, which was up a hill in an obviously affluent section. The two women drew many curious looks as they passed through the streets. Clearly, they were not the average wayfarers. Because they were women, questions doubled since women were seldom seen to travel alone. A pair of foreign women caused many raised eyebrows, especially two as exotic as this. One very tall and the other just as proportionately small, physically they were contrast enough. But each was extremely comely in her own fashion. Yet they did not carry themselves in the manner of the kind of women usually seen on the roadways alone. Neither tossed fetching glances toward the men they encountered. The buzzing of a fresh set of wagging tongues had already begun in this new place.

23

THE RICH MAN who lived in the house was known as an importer of expensive goods. His few neighbors were accustomed to being surprised by the activities at his sumptuous dwelling. Whispers of his involvement in foreign government intrigues circulated throughout the area. Though his wealth and influence were now legend, he had begun his adult life as a trader along the river route. During this time he had first met Lilith's father, who had cultivated a friendship with the young trader. Over the years, that same friendship had brought prosperity to the people of the river at the same time that it filled the coffers of this trader.

This man had watched Lilith develop into a woman that he admired greatly. Her father's acquaintance had given him a unique perspective. Because of his exposure to many cultures and castes, he was more aware than most of what she could become. The headman had sent word of his daughter's pending journey to his friend, asking for his assistance. He knew that he would have to proceed carefully. She was at a crossroads in her life, but with his help she could ascend to unbelievable heights.

The two women entered the room haltingly. Neither had seen such surroundings. Even the wedding visit had not prepared them for this. As they waited for the servant to summon their host, the pair let their senses roam about to understand all that they saw. The walls and floors were covered in skins, furs and fabrics unlike any that came from the looms of the river. Decorative bowls and urns of many varied types sat about. Furniture, the likes of which they had never seen, filled the room to a level of extreme opulence. When the host entered, he was at first overcome by Lilith's beauty. Here in this setting, it was even more apparent. He saw a tall woman of richly burnished brown color wearing clothing tailored from rust-colored skins in the suede finish common among the people of that area. The trim was of white fur and feathers, with bright blue accents. Her hair was done in the ancient braided style and the blue and white accents were made more vivid by her startling indigo blue eyes. He quickly did the mathematics in his head and determined that she was around thirty-six. Looking at her, he found it hard to believe. Her body was taut and exquisitely formed. The long legs were, by themselves, a symphony. If he had not already known that she was extremely intelligent, it would have been impossible to see beyond her beauty. He quickly noted that her companion was certainly not to be ignored. The petite woman standing beside Lilith was unknown to him. She was about the same age and another true beauty. It was certain that she stood no more than three and a half cubits high. Her eyes were the light golden color seen in some gems. They were as sharply inquisitive as they were pretty. Her body was a perfectly neat package of femininity. Her skin was the dark sand color commonly seen among the desert tribes. He had always thought the river people an interesting mix of the various tribes. This young woman was certainly not as stunning as Lilith, but she was someone that he wished to know. He welcomed them heartily and personally took each of them to the quarters that he had made available. When the two women had settled in, they tidied themselves.

After changing into sumptuous, beautifully colored robes, they joined the household for the evening meal. The room in which they ate was an oddly shaped room containing a body of water. Both women wondered how their host had obtained such a strange large bowl in which to put the water. It was almost as though a small river had been made captive. The group sat about on cushions. It had become clear that their journey was taking them further than even they had dreamed. Since the host was familiar with the world they knew, he had made a point to offer a simple meal by his standards. However, the group engaged in conversation during the meal. Unlike the gossipy village exchanges, here the topics were generalized. The women found it stimulating to be asked about their thoughts and opinions. This was especially true of Naiimi. While Lilith had been widely exposed to trade missions and the travels, Naiimi had been much more limited in her exposures. Her interests had been limited to weaving and this had been her only concern in her previous travels. Suddenly she found herself speaking out about her own feelings and was startled to hear herself do so. The host was especially attentive to her and she responded to his warmth. Since her husband had left her, she had rarely been in the close company of any men but those in Lilith's family. The scoundrels who had slipped to her door in the night certainly did not count. The headman, his sons and Adaama had all treated her much like family. Only at the wedding had she been exposed to any other men in a social situation. Naiimi found herself speaking animatedly and at length about her passion for the cloth, her daughters and myriad of other subjects that she had never known herself to care about. The host was entranced with the personable and lovely visitor.

During this time Lilith finds herself speaking with a mysterious gentleman who is also a guest in this great man's home. It seemed that he had come from the kingdom of Saba. In this fabled land of wealth and riches, this man was the confidant of great rulers. His presence at this house was not publicly known. Due to some unrest in his country, he had surreptitiously sought the counsel and assistance of the host. This meeting with Lilith, here, is one of divine chance. Years before he had seen this regal creature at a reception in the eastern city. At that time he had chosen to remain in the background. His amazement at her beauty and poise has not changed, but it is totally eclipsed by his fascination with her innate intelligence.

The astonishing evening passes under the soft flickering light of torches. The conversation, companionship and surroundings create a perfect blend. As the two women retire to chambers for the evening, they realize that even though they are exhausted, excitement will not allow them to close an eye as of yet. The pair spends several hours recounting the adventures of the evening. None of the realities of this place have sunk in. It is difficult to dissect the many and varied aspects of the evening that are totally new or surprising to them. Sleep finally overtakes the unwilling duo a few minutes before daybreak, beating them into submission. After barely five hours, Lilith's eyes pop open. She lies on the sleeping ledge, attempting to orient herself to time and location. When the details become clear to her, she is infused with adrenalin. After performing her morning routines, she is satisfied with her appearance and leaves the sleeping quarters. Upon reaching the common area of the house, she is shown to an outdoor area where the host and several others are gathered. A legion of servants move about the group, waiting upon them hand and foot. Majestic fans of feathers or palms assure the comfort of this group of dignitaries.

Lilith decides to sit and speak with the women in the group since she had limited opportunity to do so on the previous evening. A lovely woman with pale olive skin appears to read her mind and beckons to her, indicating the seat next to her. As elaborately dressed as Lilith is simply clothed, this woman has her neck, hands and ears adorned with ornate jewels. The intricate work is a puzzle to the river woman. Her eyes have not seen such craftsmanship. She cannot begin to fathom the cost of such items. During the course of the conversation, Lilith learns that the woman is the paid companion of the host. After all the years that she has heard the word 'prostitute', this is her first exposure to a woman who has made a conscious choice to lead such a life.

Despite the negative thoughts that initially crowd her mind, Lilith is interested in the woman herself. It is obvious that these people do not see her as a lesser creature. When she remembers that woman on the eastern city street years earlier, there is little common ground between this exquisite creature and that pathetic street urchin. Such a comparison amuses Lilith who wonders what the two have in common. She supposes that most obviously, both perform sexual acts for money, but the woman who sits beside her is so much more than a willing vessel. The conversation turns toward Lilith herself. Her beauty and exotic qualities are elaborated upon to the point that she becomes uncomfortable. Eventually it dawns upon Lilith that this woman is seeking to recruit her services. The tall dark woman is far more sophisticated than even she realizes. Her response is not one of anger, but one of amusement. When she rises and walks away, the host immediately goes to her side. One look at the olive-skinned woman makes him reasonably sure what has happened.

"I see that you have met Inanna." He decided to allow her to control the discussion.

An amused tinkle of laughter was Lilith's response.

"She is a woman of extraordinary loveliness and charm."

The host is especially impressed with Lilith's composure. Most women did not handle Inanna's inquiries so well. He had known that

Inanna would not be able to control her interest in the tall woman. Exotica was a marketable commodity in her trade. He had not thought that this woman would be that type, but one never knew. His mission in life was to provide people with people or things that they desired. He had long ago ceased judgments.

"She had made it clear to me that she thought the same of you. I hope that you were not insulted."

Her deep blue eyes were calculating as she replied.

"Why would I be insulted? I am not a child, sir. Perhaps my exposure has been limited, but there are few things new under the sun."

His estimate of her intelligence immediately rose to another level. "I know that you were a married woman and your opinions should have been shaped somewhat by your station in life. Most married women are intimidated by women such as Inanna. She is considered a priestess in her art by some."

"My dear man, I am a woman whose husband left her for a fresher face, though I doubt that the face was the primary source of his concern. It would be presumptuous of me to judge another woman."

"You, Lilith, are an unusual woman that is sure. Let us move to another topic. Tell me what you thought of the gentleman whom you met last evening?" He wanted to determine if his assessment of the fledgling acquaintance was correct.

She thought for a moment or two about her conversation with the distinguished man from Saba. He had been an intriguing person to meet. His handsomeness had not escaped her either. Looking around, she did not see him out on this terrace.

"He was a fascinating person to speak with. I have always been most interested in his homeland. A trader from Saba made regular stops in our village. The artifacts and jewelry that he brought were always astonishing. Perhaps one day I will travel to that land."

The host was pleased to hear her enthusiasm for even the possibility of travel to his home country. Lurking at the edges of his consciousness was the belief that her future could well lie in that very direction.

The host made sure that Lilith and her friend were treated with royal regard. All manner of goods and services were made available to them. Pampering to this degree had been beyond the imagination of the two visitors. Baths of oils and scents, laden with the sweetest of petals, became a staple in their daily routines. Among the servants were muscular young Nubian men trained to knead and pound the flesh. Once introduced to the pleasure, the women regularly availed themselves. The effect of this new life style was to polish the already well-honed beauty of both women. All traces of their long journey were erased. With glowing skin and superbly conditioned bodies, both found themselves in a sensual state of mind neither had experienced recently. Lilith likened her feelings to the period of her life after the first eastern journey. Then she was influenced by the awakened sexuality in her marriage. Now all aspects of her being were clicking into place, she was comfortable in her own skin. Her physical self was being treated to all manner of delights at the same time that her mind was being stimulated in nightly conversations with the cadre of revolving guests at the house. For the first time in her life she thought of herself as an individual first and had discovered intense joy in doing so.

Never in Naiimi's life had she experienced such a luxurious sense of self. Over the years she had channeled all of her gratification into the artistic joy she received from weaving the cloth. She had not allowed herself to be a sensual being. The fear of the ugly wagging tongues of gossip had bridled whatever desires she might have had. Suddenly she is faced with the awakening of her sensuality in a location where complete self-indulgence is possible. Forsaking the rigid braids of her past, she began to wear her hair in a loose cloud about her shoulders. The dark, thick mass of hair is less kinky than curly, allowing her a more fluid feeling of movement.

The exotic fabrics that she has created for her robes are especially flattering to her compact body and glowing skin. She becomes a joyful sprite who spends as much time singing as weaving. Daily, the host observes this woman as she unfolds into an entirely different and delightful creature than the woman who arrived at his door. He begins to look forward to her presence as the highlight of his day. Nothing takes precedence over the time he allots to spend in conversation with Naiimi. Her arranges for the master musician to provide her with training on the stringed musical instruments. Because she had already developed the easy rhythm of the loom, the stringed instrument was second nature to her. Evening salons often became the host's opportunity to entertain his many guests with performances by his lovely protégé.

The rich and powerful of the city were abuzz with the news of Naiimi. Her very name became synonymous with "pleasant". Her voice, her beauty and personality were equally soothing to all who came into her circle of influence. She was no longer the reflective moon to Lilith's sun.

As she has discovered these fresh facets of herself, so has she begun to question her feelings for the man who has made this possible. The host has been extremely

careful not to approach Naiimi prematurely. Through the many conversations he has shared with her, he sees that her past relationship has damaged her in many ways. Despite the decade's age difference between them he feels confident that their relationship is a possibility. He has carefully nurtured the friendship and been rewarded tremendously. During the past months he has felt his feelings begin to grow from amusement to something greater. In his lifetime of a little over forty-five years, he has experienced many women. First because of his travels, and later his wealth, he has chosen not to have a permanent bond with a woman. This tiny cinnamon colored sprite of a woman is changing everything in his life. He finds himself anticipating the next step in their relationship. On this evening, Lilith and the man from Saba have been invited to join some people at the home of Inanna. The host has asked Naiimi to share his evening meal. Such an occasion has never been so important to this man. His plan is not merely to seduce this woman. The purity and beauty of her soul are the ultimate prize that he wishes to share. The world as he knows it, and himself, are among the bounty that he is determined to gift upon this woman. Servants have prepared fare consisting of many delectable courses. No expense has been spared. Never in his life has he felt this way. He believes that there is a strong possibility that his feelings are shared. This dinner has to be the perfect backdrop for his declaration. When everything is as he has requested, Naiimi comes and is shown to her seat. The servants efficiently present and serve the dinner, course by course, wholly satisfying the host with the evening's progression. Naiimi senses the special tone of the dinner, but her presumption is less serious. In her mind, she flirts with the possibility that the host desires her. Somehow, it has not occurred to her that she could possibly be the woman of his dreams. She is flattered by his attention and believes that she has developed an adolescent fixation on him. As the meal draws to an end, he suggests that they move to the terrace. This man, Jahai, possesses a great degree of charm in conjunction with his natural physical attractiveness. His coffee colored skin ripples with the muscles that cover his well-proportioned torso. Whenever he sees her, a smile instantly lights his face. Naiimi feels comfortable, cherished and beautiful in his presence. When he kisses her, she is amazed by the gentle sweetness of his touch. She has been approached in many ways over the years, never with this tender regard. So it is that tenderness is the ingredient missing in her life. In this man, there is nothing of the

144

bravado she witnessed in her husband. Nowhere does she see reflected the faces of those midnight visitors to her door who sought to offer her their favors. He is not seeking to conquer her, or overwhelm her. What he accomplishes is to rouse the sexuality that has never been stirred in her. As he kisses her, Naiimi feels as though a giant flower has begun to bloom in her soul. Colors, sounds and smells become magnified beyond her experience. When the pair finally moves to his chambers, Naiimi has become the aggressor. Nothing has prepared her for the onslaught of actual desire. She had been the participant in the sexual act innumerable times with her husband. Until now, she has never initiated it. Much to the delight of the host, the petite woman has become a tigress. His gently careful touch has stoked a fire that now rages. Taking great caution, he draws her robe away from the exquisite perfection that is her body. She can see his desire for her and yet he makes no overt move to commence the act. He kneels before her, paying homage to her loveliness. By touch and kiss he covers each square inch of her body. When he finally draws her to the sleeping couch, she shifts to take the superior position. As she places her face against his massive chest, he surrounds her body in his arms. The embrace is a brief respite from the passion that has overtaken her. It also gives her the assurance that this man feels something more than lust for her. He raises her face and showers it with kisses. She is suddenly aware of her need to be filled by this man. As she makes a subtle shift of her body, she raises herself seemingly to sit on her heels. The result is her voluntary impalement. In every way she clearly chooses to take this man into her body, as well as into her heart. The host is taken beyond himself. Few women in his life have taken the innocent initiative that this tiny woman has. Her enthusiasm creates a more stimulating aura than any paid companion ever has. Setting her own pace, she rhythmically moves her body to a nearly orgiastic point. He senses, and indeed, feels her nearness. Putting his hands at her waist, they encircle her body. His thumbs meet at the center point of her back. Slowly he massages those core muscles as he slows the pace to draw her back from the edge, magnifying her pleasure. He does this repeatedly, until finally he allows her to rush the pace and they mutually collapse in sated exhaustion.

When Naiimi awakes, she is lying in his arms. Initially, she panics and then she feels the strength and comfort surrounding her. His face, buried in the mass of her hair, raises when he feels her waking.

"You sleep so beautifully. I was afraid that if I moved at all, I might disturb you."

She is a bit wary of the situation. What does she do next?

"I am sorry if I caused your discomfort." She apologized, starting to rise from the couch. He drew her back, and held her closely.

"You could never cause discomfort for me. Naiimi, surely you have been aware of my growing feelings for you. I thought that the joy that you have brought into my life was the most surprising event ever. Making love to you has magnified that joy beyond measurement."

Naiimi felt a sense of peace envelope every fiber of her being. This man had provided her first with shelter, then He had brought the best that the world had to offer through these doors. In giving her the gift of development of her talents, they had fallen in love. Tonight he had helped her to find a side of herself that she had never known existed.

Sex had been something that she had engaged in because it was expected. While she had found the experience pleasurable, it had never given her the sense of completion experienced in this man's arms tonight. The difference, she likened to her previously adolescent notions about her feelings for this man. In his arms, she had found her adult feminine self. For this she would be eternally grateful, however she was almost afraid to breathe. Surely, this was some illusion, some sensory hallucination. Remaining tentative in her response to his declaration, she murmured into his chest.

"Mmmmm, it was magnificent. But I am sure less so for you than someone of my limited experience."

He sensed the conflict in her reply and knew that the remainder of his life depended upon her understanding of his feelings and intent. It must be established here and now. Placing his hand beneath her chin, he looked directly into the sparkling topaz centers of her eyes.

"You, my small one, are the answer to everything I have been seeking in my life. The years alone have been worth it only because I have spent this short time with you. If you will consent to remain in my arms forever, my life will be completed. I love you. "

Naiimi understands that all of her senses have been operating properly, that this man truly does feel as she hoped in her heart that he might. The years spent alone no longer matter. At this moment she finally releases the memory of Bhutu's cruelty. As she encircled his neck and draws his mouth to hers, the bracelets on her arms slide into one another. Fittingly, the sound is musical.

"I have never allowed myself to dream of a man like you. If one is unaware of even the possibility that something exists, it can not be comprehended. The person that you are, was beyond the dreams of that young wife living in fear and shame between the river's branches. Even tonight, I was afraid to believe."

He hears the sincerity and truth in her voice. Somehow, it does not satisfy him. He hungers to hear her say the words that will complete their pact. It occurs to him that perhaps his own declaration was incomplete.

"Naiimi, please be afraid no longer. The sounds of the river are far away. You are safe here in my arms. Will you be my wife? I need you to be my wife. That is, if you love me."

She thought for a short moment. It did not seem like so long ago that she had deserted any thought of love or happiness with a man. But this was real. She was not deluding herself in some slumberous fantasy.

"Of course I love you. Are you absolutely certain that you wish to marry me? After all, you have had the pleasure of the legendary Inanna in your bed. But, my love, you are here and now advised that there will be no such nonsense from this day forth." With a playful growl, she tugged at his ear.

He responds affectionately, "With a wife such as you, my tiny tigress, what man could let his thoughts stray? Seriously, you should know that Inanna has been only a friend to me since the very moment that I laid eyes on you. We will marry on the evening of the full moon. Will that suit you?"

Her mind races to attempt to imagine marriage with this man. It suddenly dawns upon her that their relationship had been much that way for a while. Only the sexual component had been missing. He had cared for her and nurtured her personal growth. She had been made the jewel of his household.

"It will suit me perfectly. There is no need for delay."

With that settled, the mood became charged with desire again. This time, he led the dance and she happily followed.

Lilith observed that her friend's entire person had begun to emit some glowing quality. Even having observed her metamorphosis over the months since they had arrived, she had missed the signs. Jahai was someone that she had known for most of her life. He had spent time at the family's fire many times. She had considered him a friend of her father's, not taking into account that he was actually many years younger than the headman. Since arriving in the city, he had made their lives more comfortable than she could have dreamed. Though it had come to her notice that he was much younger than she had thought and also that he was a handsome man, it had never occurred to her that the interest he had shown in Naiimi was anything beyond kindness. When Naiimi came to her chambers the following morning, Lilith failed to see the newly vibrant aura surrounding her friend. The effervescent, bubbly woman came sweeping into the room trailing the subtle scent of fine oils in her wake.

"What do you see? Tell me, what do you see?" Her happiness was obvious.

"I see… Perhaps, that something has made you happy?" Lilith examined her friend closely. Around her neck was a magnificent necklace intricately woven of hammered gold and stones that matched Naiimi's eyes. It was more stunning than anything Lilith had seen.

"My god, Naiimi! Where did you acquire that necklace? It is amazing!"

The petite woman put her hand to her throat in a confused manner. She had forgotten the jewels that quickly.

"Oh, yes. It is beautiful, is it not? But that is not what I mean."

"Not what you mean! Naiimi, have you lost your mind?"

"Lilith, it is about me, not the jewelry!" the words came rushing out of her impatiently. She could not believe that her best friend for her whole life could not see what had happened to her.

For a few moments, Lilith took pause. Something was there. Naiimi literally resonated with joy. But she could not for the life of her, determine it's source.

"What has made you so happy?" she asked cautiously.

Naiimi could hold herself back no longer. In a torrent of giggles and laughter, she told her best friend that her soul had found its rest… That she loved this man, Jahai…that he loved her to distraction… that they would be married very shortly…and yes, finally that he had given her the necklace as a gift when she had agreed to marry him.

He had commissioned the necklace especially for her. On a trip to his jeweler some time before, he had spotted the handful of large matched stones. Because they complemented her eyes exactly, he would settle for nothing less. The jeweler had been somewhat surprised because this man had never lavished such jewelry on a woman before. He had heard whispers of the two foreign women who had lived in the rich man's home. He wondered if this was for the one referred to as the queen of the river people. Since his client wished to spare no expense, the jeweler created a necklace to suit a queen.

The household became an ant colony of preparation for the wedding. Even her daughter's wedding could not compare with the scale and grandeur that Jahai was creating for his precious ladylove. Some few had guessed about the developing relationship, but because of his bachelor past, dismissed it as one of passing amusement. With delight these people of power and substance rallied to the new couple. Naiimi's musical talent had already made her the darling of his impromptu salons. The sparks from the exquisitely passionate relationship ignited the entire circle. Love found later in life tends to infuse all who are exposed to it with the glow of shared happiness.

The wedding took place as scheduled. Lilith saw her friend join with the man who had been their host. Despite the objections of the groom, Naiimi had insisted upon personally handling the clothing she intended to wear in strict secrecy. Because he was a man accustomed to controlling his environment, he initially objected. He wished to furnish her with the finest clothing available. Finally, understanding that his bride was not going to compromise on this point, he relented graciously. Even though he was aware that she possessed no small talent for the working of the cloth, his thought was to give her everything that her heart could desire. She explained that the design and making of her bridal robe was her heart's desire and worked feverishly to complete the project. When she had designed the fabric for her daughter's gown, her thought had been to continue to make other similar patterns with thread variances. But on this occasion, her goal is to truly create her lifetime's personal masterpiece.

When she walked into the room, the sharp intake of breath that greeted her was universal. She was a vision in shimmery pale bronze fabric. Lilith knew that she had used an unusually dense numbers of threads to create the effect. The color was perfect complement to her skin, her eyes and the necklace that her new husband had given her. Naiimi had the look of an exquisitely crafted object of finest quality. Not a single raw or unrefined quality hovered about the woman who presented herself on this evening. Her mature beauty and vivacity emitted a glow that was apparent to all who witnessed.

The city wedding festivities did not stretch out for the days as provincial ones tended to do. By the time that word of the richness of both the feasts, and of the groom, made its way to the river, the few guests had returned to inform the wagging tongues in person. Lilith's brothers had made the journey, as much to see their sister as to attend the wedding. The headman and Hana had not felt that they should attempt such a long journey in such a short time. They had sent their good wishes to dear friends. Naiimi's youngest daughter and her new husband came to provide that family's blessings. They also brought word of the grandson born to her oldest at the summer's end. Everyone who knew Naiimi bore extraordinary sense of thanks for the happiness that she had finally found for herself. Each of them knew what her journey had been to come to this place in her life. No one could have predicted her triumph over such obstacles.

When the symptoms first appeared, Naiimi was totally unaware. She was a healthy vibrant and happy woman of thirty-seven summers. This marriage was the most amazing thing that had happened in her life. She noticed the cessation of her moon flow, but she attributed it to her age. By the time that her body began to thicken slightly, it hit her. She had felt a slight soreness in her breasts, but had thought with a warm flush that her husband's attention to them must have been excessive. There had not been a single episode of the morning agonies that she had endured with her past child bearing. Her daughters had been born when she was barely past adolescence. Carrying each of

them had been a horror for her. Her quick count told her that she had
to be well past the first third of the child- bearing phase.

Immediately, her concern was to determine what her husband's
feelings might be. After all, she was the mother of grown up daughters. He had no children that she had been made aware of. How would
he feel? He was in his forties, vigorous and full-blooded still, but...
As she sat on the terrace contemplating their situation, he came out.
When she had awakened this morning, he had already departed for
a meeting. The day had not yet reached its mid point and he had returned. She rose to greet him with an embrace.

"Darling, I did not expect that you would return so quickly."

"How could I not when I know that you await me here?"

As the couple stood there embracing in the morning sunlight,
Naiimi's mind rushed forward, wondering what his reaction to her
news might be. She took his hand and led him to one of the many
couches placed about the terrace.

"I think that I need to tell you something. This is difficult because
it had never occurred to me that..."

When she paused, he first began to worry. He could think of
nothing that might give him any problem in his life now. Only if she
should cease loving him would he see anything as an obstacle. He had
to stop his mind from creating mad scenarios. He interrupted her.

"You can tell me anything. You should know that."

When the words came out of her mouth, it was as though he
heard the pieces of the heavens fall properly into place.

He had noticed the subtle changes in her precious body, but his
head had overruled his heart. She tended to work at her music or her
loom with passionate zeal, often forgetting to eat. He had thought
she had begun to thicken slightly because he had been guilty of constantly plying her with food and exotic treats. But, instead they were
expecting a child?? His heart began to thump wildly. He took a breath

and looked at her. He placed his hand upon the sweet swell of her abdomen.

"When you agreed to marry me I had thought that nothing else could ever make me so happy. Then on the night we married you were a like a precious candle. The fire contained within was mine alone to enjoy. But now you give me a gift that I had never thought to receive in this lifetime."

Tears pooled unashamedly in his eyes and the salty taste of his tears mingled with hers as they kissed.

Her term continued in the vein with which it had begun. She only knew by the rounded swell of her belly that she was going to bear a child. The flutters and kicks were pleasant reminders of the baby's presence. Her husband treated her even more regally. Servants waited on her hand and foot from dawn to dusk. He took a great deal of pride in performing tasks for her. Somehow she seemed to be rendered incapable of bathing herself or dressing herself alone. If he had not been so endearing, she might have become annoyed.

She often joked with him that she felt like the sacrificial animal in some temple. Her only concern was that because she was having such a beautiful term, the altar of childbirth might be her undoing. He heard her concern and took it to heart.

A pair of specially trained midwives was brought in to assist her. They began by the daily massaging of oils into her skin. Her body had not distended badly and they assured her that these unguents would prohibit the distortion of her skin and muscles as the baby grew. Naiimi questioned what must have been an exorbitant expense. At the same time she did begin to feel more confident.

These women had prepared her private birthing room at the rear of the house. It was difficult to believe the degree of activity centered around the birth of a single baby. Her fears lessened as her well being continued. In the last few days before her baby was due, she began to worry that something had to go wrong. She was healthy. Her husband was a gift from the gods. Her life was hard to believe, even now. When she woke up in tears, her husband consoled her as best he could. The thought had also occurred to him that it was, all indeed, too perfect. At this stage of life he had learned to view everything with some skepticism. Naiimi had come along and changed his world. A child, a precious heir, was almost too good to hope for. He told himself that she was healthy and his only concern was keeping her that way. The morning that she felt the slight twinge in her back, she thought that perhaps she had slept improperly.

Her prior labors had been brutal both in onset and duration so she could not have imagined that her labor had begun. When the servant brought her food, she inquired after her husband and only picked over the sumptuous offering of fruits and the hot grain dish that she preferred. He walked into the bedchamber with a giant smile across his face. In his hand was a box carved of marble, perched upon a pillow. Her reaction was that of a child who has been overfed. He never stopped bringing her trinkets regardless to how many times she told him that enough was enough. As she lifted the lid another twinge hit her. Inside the box was a ring. The topaz stone was encased in a cage of gold in the same design as her wedding necklace. She had to admit that this was no mere trinket. As he slipped the jewel onto her finger, he kissed her hand.

"You have given my life color that I had no idea existed.

Before you, I was a blind man who was not aware of his infirmity. Thank you for bringing the light to my life."

She was touched by his constant reaffirmation. As she placed her hands on each side of his face, a sharper twinge started at either side of her spine and circled below her stomach. Blinking her eyes, she made a sharp intake of breath.

"My dear husband I believe that the event is here."

He swept her up into his arms and rushed her to the birthing room. As she heard the scuff of his sandaled feet rushing her through the halls, her mind was filled with fearful anticipation. Entering the birth chamber, she saw that preparations were already under way. Steamy air rose from the coals. Stacks of linen sat in waiting. The birthing chair carved from a precious wood sat waiting in its pristine glory. He lowered her to the couch and allowed the midwives to do the job that they had been brought here to do. The duo efficiently examined and bathed her simultaneously. They rubbed potions into her birth canal that were said to ease the labor process. One of the women led the expectant father from the inner chamber, explaining that it was best that he not be at the center of the activities. Despite his age, they reminded him, he was still a first time father. When the woman left him, he felt useless. His assurance was that he had provided the best possible surroundings for his beloved wife. He only prayed that the gods understood what this woman meant to him.

When the midwife examined Naiimi, she was shocked to see that instead of just beginning labor, the petite woman was in the most advanced stage. The husband had let the two women know that his wife had some fear due to her previous experience. Quickly one of the midwives placed her on the birthing chair and gave her the drink that they had prepared. Certain herbs had been found to ease the throes of labor and help the mother to be relax. Naiimi heard the women say that her labor was advanced however it was hard for her to believe this. Yes, she felt the pain. But it was not of the body wracking jolts that had plagued her early before. She prayed continually for the health and well being of her child. In the darkest recesses of her mind she worried that something had to be wrong. It must be that the child is too small to survive, or that it has died. Her belief was that her small body could not possibly bear a child comfortably. Her thought was more for her husband than herself. She already had children, two fine daughters.

Before she knew what had happened, the final pain came rushing to its apex. There was a sudden jolt and she heard the exclamations of the midwife.

"The gods be praised! Look at him!"

When she realized that they were referring to her child, Naiimi was afraid. Why didn't she hear him cry? Before she could say the actual words, A loud and lengthy wail quieted her fear. Her baby was alive. But was he well? Was he whole?

"Madam, Sir," the woman called out excitedly. "The baby is a big healthy boy!" She spoke in a quieter tone directly to Naiimi. "Madam, his father will be proud!"

As the second midwife took care of her needs, the first promptly washed the baby and took him out to the proud father for viewing. Impatiently, Naiimi awaited her turn to see her son. It was hard to believe that this had happened so easily.

The minor amount of pain was nothing compared to the birthing of the girls. As her life had taken this fortunate turn, it had done so on all fronts. When she was cleaned and ensconced on the sleeping couch that had been put in the room, the midwife brought her baby. Naiimi was able to assure herself that all ten fingers and toes were in place. Her husband hovered about. He needed to see for himself that she had done as well as the midwives had said. The baby was a precious gift, but one secondary to the well being of his wife.

As the plump little boy was placed in her arms, Naiimi saw that he was indeed a big healthy boy. He had the rich dusky skin tones of her husband. His features were perfect and beautiful. She could not believe her blessings. The gods had heard her prayers, all of them.

When Lilith was told of the impending birth, she had rushed to the home of the new parents. After the host had proposed to her friend, Lilith had decided that she needed to give the couple privacy. Over their objections she had located suitable lodgings not too far from them. When the servants had come to her door, Lilith had not paused in following them back. She too offered prayers to all the gods of the river people. The superstitions that Naiimi had expressed were very much hers also. Nothing in the shared history of these two women had allowed the luxury of such complete happiness. Surely there was a price to be exacted. But the fat, healthy, little boy had already come into the world when she arrived. Her friend was hale, hearty, happy beyond belief and only slightly tired. Everything was even better than she could have prayed for or imagined. Naiimi's journey had come to the most perfect conclusion. Fate had shown her the other side of her coin.

24

Start all

LILITH HAD SPENT the recent years in the great city continuing to function as an ambassador of her people. She had met many people of influence and moved among the various capitols. Everywhere she was given the respect accorded royalty. From the time of her birth, Lilith's father had secreted away a cache of ivory to secure his daughter's station in life. If her marriage had become an issue, he might have been forced to offer most of it as a bride price. Since she had married a local lad, this had not been the case. After Adaama's desertion, he had presented this treasure to her. Lilith was initially awed that her father had done such a thing for her. It was not an entirely unusual practice, but because so much time had passed since her marriage, she was caught totally unaware. A myriad of the intricately carved ivory pieces that he had bought and traded for, lay in a finely wrought basket that Hana had weaved before her birth. His thought was to offer her the cushion she might need to go forward with her life. Once he had presumed that he would present this bounty to she and her husband at some point. For some reason unknown to him, he had held back year after year as he continued to fatten the treasure.

When Lilith told him of her desire to travel, he knew that the time had come to provide his daughter with the ability to see the world as she chose, on her own terms. A portion of the sums had been sent to his trusted old friend, the host, to hold for her safely. Similar arrangements were made in other locations to cushion his daughter's way. Those who thought her to be a queen were not completely mistaken. This woman was as wealthy, as beautiful and as well connected as any in her time. She was a queen in search of a kingdom worthy of her.

Among the people with whom she had become closely associated, was the mysterious man from Saba that she met on her first evening in the home of Jahai. After his conversations with Lilith that first evening, he had approached his host and confidante.

"Tell me about the tall woman, the one that is referred to as the Queen of the river people."

Even though the host knew that his friend appreciated her beauty, he knew that her beauty was only a small component

of his interest. The former trader told the man Lilith's story as only a family friend would. Her family's influence extended well beyond the borders of their kingdom. Despite their modest daily lives, her family possessed great wealth. Many men in his time and sphere of influence respected the headman's counsel and status. This woman clearly was born to royal lineage. It was no myth that she was called the "Queen of Smargados". The kingdom of the water was as real as any. Her father had long ago abdicated

the administrative duties of his kingdom to this oldest child. Her residence in this city had become the kingdom's headquarters. Whenever her people were dispatched to the city for trading purposes, she was available to assist them in any regard.

After that fateful first meeting, this man from Saba spent much time with Lilith. He told himself that the friendship was a purely intellectual exercise. He was an admirer of strong women and preferred their company. But there was another long buried truth. This very tall man had long harbored an acutely personal interest in her. It was a natural step that he invited her to visit the realm that is his present homeland. While visiting, she is accorded all the hospitality that his kingdom can muster. Since the kingdom of the river people has long traded with Saba, the two people have many cultural commonalities. Lilith blends easily into the society. Her mentor is as impressed with her behavior and carriage in his country, as he was at their first meeting. She makes the very long trek to accomplish several extended visits to his homeland.

An idea had begun to take root in this man's mind. His kingdom currently suffers a void in leadership. The leader is dying and has no heirs. One of the primary reasons that this distinguished citizen of Saba had visited in the home of the host at that moment was to begin to determine the course of his country's future. This man, once a warrior prince now a merchant, is now one of the members of a wealthy shadow government that had existed for decades. Once he was informed that Lilith had the assets to couple with her intelligence and personal magnetism, his decision is made. She is a natural person to draw into this established conspiracy. Her popularity extends down to the masses. Already legend in this land, her beauty has continued to captivate the imaginations of all that see her. Her appearance is now more carefully crafted, than at any stage of her life. Clothing has become an essential element in her life, as part of the shield she uses to separate her inner self from the world. Her beauty is the mask she uses to shield her pain. Exposure to many cultures has honed her appetite for dramatic attire. The clothiers of the city added a few particularly exciting items to her wardrobe. One of the favorites was a majestic cape constructed from feathers and fur, a grandiose garment crafted by the same artisans who clothed the royal family. When she donned the feathered wrap to visit one of the outer areas of the country on a chilly day, the primitive folk mistook it for wings. She has become a creature larger than life. The wagging tongues keep everyone aware that she has neither remarried nor taken a lover. Men fantasize about the sensual possibilities of her perfect unavailable femininity. With wealth, beauty, mystery and power as her aphrodisiacs, the kingdom becomes enamored of this foreign woman, this Lilith.

Indeed Lilith is the favorite subject of the wags. Though she claims to ignore their attention, her behavior is often governed by what might be said. She has been a political being since birth. Why would she change now?

At the death of the reigning leader, the shadow government places Lilith on the throne. The Queen of the water (Zmargad) is now the Queen of Saba. The borders of this land are extended across the water to include the kingdom of the river people. A portion of the mighty Red Sea is now completely enfolded into the boundaries of her new home. Saba is poised to become the greatest kingdom in the known world with Lilith at its head.

The mysterious man who brought Lilith to power, Samael, is her constant companion. Since their meeting she realizes that he has become an integral part of her life. Of all people, he has the most constant access to her person. His counsel has been invaluable to her. Lilith finds that she eagerly looks forward to his presence. Since she has been alone for so long, she is wary of caring about another man. Instinctively, she senses his feelings for her, however he has failed to express any personal sentiments.

As time passes, she realizes that though this country has become her home, she has no friends except him. She has not a single female ear into which she can whisper her heart's concerns. Never has she been more alone. Even though she is happy for her dear friend, Naiimi's presence is truly missed. One day she hoped that the new family might come to visit her here. It is out of the question that she leave her new kingdom at any time soon since the political climate remains slightly unstable.

Lilith realizes that she knows nothing of Samael's personal life. Even after having spent considerable time in his home, she can only presume that he too is alone in life. The quarters were all quite private, so realistically he could have had an entire harem ensconced in a far section of his home. His piercing gaze gives her no clues as to his feelings. This was the one time in her life that she might have sought out the whispers of the wagging tongues of gossip. If only she had some idea of what his life was. In his eyes, she saw a wall of sorts. There was some kind of deep emotional pain in his past, she was sure. It occurred to her that they would be a perfectly matched, albeit damaged, set. Her own past must surely reflect in her eyes. The pain of Adaama's abandonment still lay heavily upon her heart. At times she has wondered where he and the girl had settled. Rumors had circulated that they had taken a northerly route seeking to remove themselves from the harshness of the sun in the lower climes. By now, she thought, they had children. The girl was young, so they had probably produced half a dozen by now, Lilith thought spitefully. She seldom allowed herself to descend to such lows. It was her current emotional unrest about Samael that was bringing these thoughts to the surface of her mind. Other men generally gave her a great deal of attention, so she knew that she was still as attractive to them as she had been. Only Samael remained the enigma. Perhaps she no longer knew the proper manner in which to signal her interest. Flirting had never been her strong suit. On the one occasion in her life that she had consciously flirted, her husband had been in the process of the ultimate betrayal. It had left a bitter taste in her mouth. She had not made a single playful gesture toward the opposite sex since then. Things were going to have to change if she was going to obtain this man's affection. Lilith felt silly planning a campaign to get a man's attention, when she had a nation to rule. Her sense of responsibility remained as staunch as during those days she dutifully walked the length of the village with her father. But the years being alone had taken their toll and she was determined to end her solitude. Lilith knew that she needed to learn more about him as a first step. Surely as Queen, any information should be hers. A source would have to be located.

Lilith began to consciously pay attention to everything he did and said. Any preferences that he uttered were noted in the mental file that she was creating. She listened when he expressed interest in anything about her. When he complemented her on her appearance in a particular red robe, the royal tailor was immediately dispatched to duplicate the garment in question by cut, then also to create other designs in the same color. The staff of tailors had to be doubled temporarily. The palace was buzzing with talk of the queen's vanity and extravagance.

Despite her increased friendliness and availability, he continued to treat her as a colleague. Season after season passed and still none of her tactics were successful. Her friend Naiimi's son was now past four years old. In desperation, Lilith decided that the only way to get this man was to seduce him. Having no real experience in such matters, she utilized immense resources in her effort. An elaborate plan was created for a romantic dinner. Without his knowledge, the dinner was to be totally private. Since they often shared meals, she only had to arrange to have her servants away. Days of preparation went into the plan. When the evening finally arrived, the ruse worked without any problems. They shared a delicious dinner in her private quarters. Each course was specifically chosen to heighten the senses. She poured cup after cup of a heady wine selected because of its strength. Her own barriers needed to be relaxed as much as she sought to lower his. As the evening grew unusually late, their conversation slowed to more smiles than words. She noticed that he seldom used both sides of his mouth when he smiled. Most often only one side of his face partic-ipated. In her state of early intoxication she saw that when he was truly amused, two deep circles appeared in each of his cheeks. Then the shadows also disappeared from his eyes momentarily. It was no effort for her to concentrate on amusing him. She regaled him with story after story of some of the unique characters along the river and of her childhood adventures. They sat about on cushions and laughed. She allowed the torches to burn down deliberately low. A moment came, when she could not resist but reach out and touch one of his dimpled cheeks. As her graceful fingertip traced a line toward his lips, he grasped her hand gently and covered her palm in kisses. At her wrist, his lips paused to linger at the delicate point of her pulse. The stimulating aroma of an exotic oil titillated his nostrils as he lingered lovingly, licking and teasing the sweet skin of her wrist. Literally mak-ing love to her hands, each fingertip was tasted, kissed and massaged in turn. Once the task was complete, he moved his lips up her arms in a tantalizingly slow fashion. Pausing at the bends of her arms to again stimulate pulse points, he had created a buzzing sensation in her body. Lilith, in her slightly intoxicated state, felt that her body had become an unknown entity. It had never occurred to her that the skin was one giant erogenous zone. By the time that he gently placed his fingertips on the very tips of her breasts, her entire body had begun to vibrate. It was as though her body was the finely crafted instrument he used to create music never before heard by the human ear. When he pulled the strings to disrobe her, Lilith felt a sense of delight in every fiber of her being. She was aware that he remained clothed, but lost all reason-able thought when he lowered his mouth to her breasts. Her pleasure was the sole purpose of this sensual journey, as though he was clearly aware that her body had been sexually starved for too long. She had transferred her physical desires into other forms of gratification. Now she was being rewarded beyond measure. Never in her wildest dreams had she imagined such bliss could exist. His only purpose seemed to be to salaciously explore each and every single square inch of her body. Samael took his lips away from her breasts and she thought that she would cry. Then his fingers replaced them as he descended the length of her body with the softest of kisses. As she lay sprawled on the cushions, her delirious thought was that she was merely another course of the feast. His magical fingertips traveled to the insides of her taut and glorious thighs. He had long admired the sleek perfection of her limbs. But even his imagination had not done them justice. He massaged them rhythmically, but gently and slowly. Not a single movement was rushed or premature. Just as she thought she might faint from the anticipation, his fingers gently began to graze her most private area. In the back of her mind Lilith continued to expect that at some point soon he would stop his attention to her. As her pleasure began to crescendo, he still did not move his body to enter her for his own gratification. When her body began to spasm in earnest, she heard herself howling like some wild creature. Wave after fantastic wave racked her core and her mind floated to some unexplored plane of pleasure. As sleep took over her exhausted body, her only thought was one of joyful gratitude.

Blinding rays of sunlight flooded her chambers. Just as she opened her eyes, she became aware of the dream from which she had emerged. It had been a sequel to the horrible dream she had experienced after Adaama had gone. Only this time, it began when everyone had abandoned her. Samael had come. He had patiently tended to her and healed her. When he lifted her up into his arms to carry her away, the sunshine had come from behind the dark cloud. She looked around her and saw that the blue mountain flowers were suddenly carpeting the entire area. She woke up to the sweet memory of their piquant aroma. It was clear that he must have carried her from the cushions to the sleeping couch last night before he left. As the memories flooded her senses, her body felt faint echoes of the joyous satisfaction. She wondered for a moment if he had taken his own pleasure when putting her to bed. Then she realized that her body would have shown signs. She had not known that such an unselfish man existed. It was strange to find such fulfillment after all these years alone. But it was odd that he had not at least stayed to resume their lovemaking this morning. Stretching her limbs luxuriously, the thought crossed Lilith's mind that on this day she felt that her body was now in tune with her mind. She made the decision that Samael had given her an invaluable gift and she was simply thankful. The time would come for her to provide his share of pleasure soon.

Before she could complete her morning toilette, her female servant came into the chamber, her head bowed. In her hand she bore an engraved gold colored box.

"Good Morning Her Royal Majesty. This was delivered for the Queen's pleasure. You were to be given this as soon as you were awake."

The girl was apologetic and obviously fearful that she had not followed her instruction. Lilith did not believe in mistreating her servants. She had lived most of her life without them and certainly understood work.

"Do not worry, you came just as I opened my eyes. You did nothing wrong."

Lilith extended her hands to accept the box. Who knew what this contained. The head manservant usually examined all gifts before they came to her hands. Precautions had to be taken in such a volatile political climate. Rulers were often dispatched through the guise of gifts containing poisonous serpents and their like. Having grown up in a benign society, it was quite an adjustment to understand the rules here. Upon closer examination, the golden box was not gilt, but actually fashioned from that most precious of metals. Fitting nicely into the hand, it was of equal breadth and depth. On the surface was carved a continuous design that was inlaid with jewels. Even when considering the treasures she had possession of as the Queen of this land, this was an impressive item. Once she finally absorbed the value of the box, it dawned upon her that she should open it. Because of the magnificence of the container, she could not fathom what the contents might possibly be. Very gingerly she raised the heavy lid. Nestled inside an embroidered silken lining was a single unset jewel. The size of this stone alone made it legend. Its color was the rich color of blood transfused with light. Cradling it in her hands, Lilith could not imagine where such a thing could have originated. It seemed almost alive. Disappointedly, the Queen noticed that the servant girl had gone from the room. Holding it up to the light she wished that she had someone to share it with. As she stood transfixed, there was a slight rustling sound behind her.

"It appears to have a life of it's own. Does it not?" Samael stood there. His face was as serious as ever.

"Are you responsible for this?" A smiling Lilith was taken aback by his grave countenance. After the intimacy they had shared, how could he be so solemn this morning? Where was his joy?

"Yes, I am. This stone is representative of life itself. The color could not be more like blood. I wanted you to have it because you represent life to me." His face maintained the grave expression.

Lilith was touched beyond measure. His seriousness was sincere. She placed the stone in its precious container. Moving quickly, she ran to embrace him passionately. He kissed her hungrily and deeply. Samael was a broad shouldered man of large stature. The deep tan of his complexion was contrasted by the rich russet shade of his hair. He was even taller than her husband had been. His arms were as powerful as his hands and lips were gentle. He was a man of extreme contrasts. His powerful physique was tempered by the bright crescent of his beautiful smile. His intellect was as mighty a weapon as a sword was in his hands. His reputation as a warrior was legend. She had discovered that he had begun his life as a servant to a cruel master. Stories were murky about his beginnings, but he had somehow won his freedom along with a nest egg of sorts. He began acquisition of his wealth through shrewdly trading for a few years. Living frugally, he continually re-invested his entire holdings until he had amassed a genuine fortune. Through the contacts he made brokering luxury items he had become one of the most powerful men in the country.

Samael held Lilith in his arms and prayed to his gods. Never in his life had he wanted or expected to receive the love and understanding of a woman. From childhood his survival had been the product of his quick mind and physical endurance.

She was happy to see him and to feel the comfort of his arms. His mood this morning was very somber, but she thought that it was the portent of something good. It seemed that he was seeking assurance from her. She encircled his neck with the graceful columns of her arms.

Remembering what he had made even her arms feel on the previous evening caused small tremors to run the length of her spine.

"Is there some symbolic reason that you give me a jewel that represents blood?" She kept her tone light and bantering.

"Yes, Lilith. If you can accept me as I am. I will give you anything in my power...anything that you think you need for happiness... I will try to fill your every heart's desire."

"You speak as though I am some capricious girl. Samael, I am a woman full grown. Remember? My heart seeks no more than what we have already found. The length of time that it took for you to recognize my yearning for you was painful."

"It was not that I did not feel the call of your heart to mine. These years have been painful for me, too. There are other things that you must know. It is not so simple."

Lilith could not believe that he was still so unsure of her feelings. What could she do to make him understand? She tried once more.

"What do you wish me to know? Just tell me."

A cloudy scowl replaced the look on his face. There was something important. Lilith saw the shadows of pain return to his eyes. She saw him consciously try to look less forbidding.

"It is not a simple thing. But it is the story of my life."

He touched her face. The thought was in his head that the ungodly shock of her eyes only served to make her more beautiful. He needed this woman to understand and not reject him out of hand. Making love to her had been like nothing before in his life. He took a deep breath and plunged forward.

"My life began under less than humble circumstances. I was one of many children born on my master's land. I believe that I know who my mother was, but I never knew my father. My master took a special liking to me when I was a small boy. There were a half dozen of us that were treated differently. We were fed well and given the best of everything. Our duties were to wait on the master hand and foot. He seemed to take a delight in hand feeding us, stroking our hair and faces. There was always one who was especially favored. Usually a bit older than the rest of us, he was never allowed to leave the master's side. As small children, we only relished our positive turn of fate.

The older we became, the more we understood and the more ominous our condition became. Generally we were separated from the other servants, his beautiful corps of companions. In truth we were all, really, slaves. He became ill finally. His mind, as much as his body, became infirm. As the master began to lose his grip on reality, his key servants began to take advantage of the current circumstances.

We were exposed to the other servants at times and they took relish in explaining what the master truly was. About this time, I was nine years or so. The favored boy took suddenly ill and died. The old master was distraught, beside himself with grief. He needed an immediate replacement for the pet boy. We were paraded before him naked in the middle of the night… A half dozen little boys, quaking with fear. As my odd coloring set me apart, I was the one he thought most desirable. The chief servant took me to the old woman who delivered babies and tended the sick. I can still smell the potions that brewed and bubbled in the hovel where she lived."

He stopped to summon the courage to continue. He looked away from her face. The recounting was too painful and he did not wish to see the horrified look that she must have on her face. Lilith was not horrified, only confused. Nothing in her cultural background prepared her for his story. She only wanted to take away his hurt. She took his hands in hers and kissed them as he spoke again.

"I was tied to the couch and cut. My master was a catamite who chose to keep the favored boy as young as possible, for as long as possible." The tears poured down his face unashamedly. "The old man wished to remove that which would make his boys change, but he thought it smart to maintain the basic equipment. Perhaps it was his source of interest. Luckily, the old woman was either not as good at her job as she had been in the past, or the gods intervened on my behalf. Despite the horrendous scars and suffering, she missed a portion of her target. I am not like other men, but I was not made an eunuch. The old woman did not remove all of that which makes me a man."

Lilith's heart bled to hear the shame and pain in his voice. While she did not totally understand every implication of his story, she knew that she loved him.

His courage and strength of character endeared him to her more so. The image of that damaged and bleeding boy saturated her senses.

She continued to kiss his hands, which by now, were covered in her tears. He spoke at a slower pace now.

"The gods did indeed smile on me. While I lay healing, the old master took very ill. He never regained his former state, but lay ailing for years on death's doorstep. Our little group of pet boys grew up unharmed. The chief servant in his household felt it necessary to maintain the household as though our master were well. When the old man died, each of us was given a few coins. Before anyone of substance knew that he had gone, all of the servants had disappeared. By then I had begun to grow up. I found menial work first. Then I stumbled upon an opportunity to soldier for money. We were trained intensely. Since I was bigger and stronger, I was good at the tasks. My skill grew, as did my reputation. From one place to the other, I was a military vagabond. Time after time, I signed on to fight wars and added to my hoard of coins until it grew. Nothing could deter me from my mission. My experience taught me early that I could not belong to another ever again. The injuries that I had suffered eliminated early interest in women because I could not rid myself of the shame. Only years later, when I could afford to pay for their companionship, did I approach any woman. You are the first woman that I have ever loved. I have desired you from the moment that I laid eyes on you many years ago. But I will hold no malice in my heart if you can not accept me as I am."

Lilith looked up directly into the shadowed eyes. Her eyes were overflowing with tears. She was not one hundred percent sure what to do next, but it was clear that he needed emotional and physical assurance. It was her task to provide it, however unsure she was about the next steps. She took him by the hand and led him to the lushly appointed sleeping couch. She sat him down and put her fingers to his lips, shushing any further words... After locking her door to any possible intrusion, she walked back to the couch removing her robes.

Samael's eyes were widened. If He had not been sure of her intent, it was now clarified. She removed his sandals first, then each piece of his clothing in turn.

Unwinding his loin covering last. She hoped that his scars were not such that she would appear repulsed. It was imperative that she be everything he needed her to be at this moment. The cloth fell away, but Lilith saw no real difference on the surface. She touched him. He tried unsuccessfully to push her hand away. Her hand moved between his thighs to touch him gently. Here, she found his shame. A dense network of scars seemed to anchor his member. On one side the scarring was much worst. On the other side his fullness curved normally beneath him. His response to her touch was extraordinarily normal. When she did not recoil from him, but continued to softly stroke and touch him, Samael knew that he was blessed. The scars were a testament to an agonizing past that she intended to wipe away. She had the need to give him what he had never before experienced. Her penchant for the superior position came flooding back. Lilith swung astraddle him. First she clasped his thighs between her knees, rocking back and forth teasing him. Unable to restrain herself any longer, she moved forward and took him into her body. He allowed her complete control. She used him as her instrument, creating harmonies to please them both. When the last shudder tore through him, he had no doubts. She was his one true love. Two damaged individuals had been blessed enough to find one another. Her injured heart had finally found its resting place. A scarred body was no longer a reason for him to feel repulsive and be alone. Together, Lilith and Samael were made whole.

The wagging tongues by now had caught wind of the love shared by this pair. Each of them had provided fodder for the wags for many years. Whispers of Samael's injuries had quietly found many an eager ear. The stories had been exaggerated more so because of his heroic status and wealth. His solitary life had only lent credence to the rumors.

Men did not usually survive castration and retain physical interest in woman. To later obtain the love of a woman such as this queen was unheard of and many thought, unnatural. Lilith's history did nothing to quell the rumors. Her extravagant beauty had been reason enough for the level of interest in her life. She was a woman who had been rejected and abandoned. Her bed remained unfilled, but her vanity intact. This was an affront to a burgeoning patriarchal society. Love between two such people was tantamount to heresy. It would prove their undoing.

Samael and Lilith joined in marriage just as they had partnered politically. He was closer than an ally, more her other half. He was Warrior Prince to his beloved Queen.

Their tandem rule allowed all segments of their lives to be joined. It was a love that was meant to be. By day the ship of state was their vessel of choice. Their nights were devoted to negotiating the seas of passion. Each of them had lived too long without sensual pleasures. It was clear to the servants that the union of this pair could not be focused on procreation. Equally apparent was their focus on sensual pleasure. The whispers emanated from the palace servants straight to the waiting ears of the wags who passed along their limited understanding of this union.

Just as Lilith had been reported to have wings in the past, their joy in the bedchamber was misinterpreted. Since the master was reported to be castrated, who could possibly be in such romps with the queen night after night? To further insult them, days were not off limits to this loving pair. The primitive answer was the involvement of some mysterious third party, named by the licentious queen herself as Blind Dragon. None used their imagination to correctly interpret this pet name for the prince's majestic member. Thus the rumors were further heightened. The royal couple was oblivious to the whispers of the wagging tongues.

25

MANY YEARS HAD passed, since the chilly morning when the two women had separated from the group on that mountain pass. When Lilith left the home of her childhood, returning was not something she had thought about. The primary focus of her concern was to get into the world. Happiness had began to create some sense of nostalgia for the Queen. More than anything she wished for her family to know that her heart had truly found it's home. While she had passed messages to them, she had seen not one of her blood relatives in a very long time.

Rumors had placed her older son in the outer reaches of her kingdom, but she was not sure that she even wished to see him. His life was one that skirted the edges of decency with a reputation as that of a dangerous man who killed with little to no provocation. No one was ever willing to say that he lacked justification since his ability to instill fear in those around him had served him well. Her younger son lived the quiet life of a carver in the village. Word had been sent of his marriage and the subsequent birth of a son.

Both of her brothers had come east to the marriage of Naiimi. It had been a wonderful visit at that time, but too many years had passed since. Lately, her constant thought had been of her parents. Now she knew that level of devotion shared by Hana and the headman. It suddenly occurred to her to wonder why her father was not called King. Until now, it had never been something that had been of interest. But then, she had not known of her father's wealth and influence until recent years. That he was respected by many outside his home village had been clear. Perhaps the lives of the people in the river kingdom had not demanded royalty at that time. Now she was their Queen, as they were a part of the Kingdom of Saba. But for some reason the outside world had always referred to her as Queen. She had been unsure back then. Now she had become accustomed to, and relished, the trappings of royalty. For a moment she considered some royal decree or proclamation that would bring her family to her.

As she sat in her throne room on this day, matters of state were far from her mind. Samael had been out to speak with a troublesome group of priests. The old ways were changing and many religious sects were springing up about the kingdom. Most troublesome were the converts to the Judean god. For some reason many of these men regarded her as an affront to their very existence. Samael had no patience for these men, but she wished to keep civil discord at a minimum. Since they did not want to deal with a woman, she sent her husband as her ambassador. His very presence was formidable. As a warrior, he had been dubbed the Angel of Rome. His heroics in the defense of that foreign city had been chronicled about the known world. When he walked into a room, every person in the room deferred to him. His stature and carriage alone brought fear to the hearts of many.

For her, his presence made her heart sing. He had made her finally feel loved and cherished. It was a constant private amusement that some thought him to be less than a man. Power and wealth along with his reputation as a warrior had long ago eliminated any public questions. The whispers had persisted as much out of fear as knowledge. An aura of danger surrounded him.

He strode confidently, quickly into the throne room. A smile crossed his face at the sight of his wife.

"Her Highness," he knelt and kissed her hand. "I have important news for you."

Lilith rose and took his hands in hers. She felt that she had made him appear by thinking of him.

"Is this news for the court to hear? Or should we retire to chambers?"

She was bored after a morning of the most mundane type of government business. A private afternoon would be a welcome alternative. He chuckled under his breath. She was extremely transparent at times.

"Actually, the news is not of a personal nature."

A look flashed like lightning between them. The game was afoot. His teasing was obvious and she was about to become impatient. He knew that she wanted to leave here at this moment, but he wished to surprise her without any sensual distraction. He wanted to see the look on her face when he told her.

Lilith lifted one eyebrow in a haughty fashion. Her voice became noticeably cool as she dropped his hands.

"Does this concern the priests?"

"No, your highness, it does not. I have made arrangements for a state visit of extreme importance."

Her second eyebrow took a quizzical arch. At this moment in time, the last thing on her list of desires was to play hostess to some fat little man from the outer reaches of Nowhere. Neither did she wish to travel, even in royal comfort, to the outer reaches of Nowhere. Her thought was that she needed to retire to her chambers alone at this very moment. That way she could avoid the entire process.

If he never told her, then she would not offend anyone by refusing to go. A sense of royal responsibility overtook her. She wondered what was wrong with her head today.

"Of course. I am sure that the visit is one that we will also find rewarding. Who is the personage who is to visit?"

Sitting back down, she had used her most sovereign voice and manner. At this point her day was already a minus. She tried to sound as though she cared. Nothing was pressing them diplomatically. The primary issues of concern were domestic. His smile was a bit disconcerting. He was so unlike himself today.

"The visit, my Queen, is one of state. You are to make a visit... a visit to the most loyal of your provinces. The arrangements have been finalized just today."

She was a little perturbed that he had done something like this with out her knowledge. Again, he was totally out of character today.

"Nothing comes to mind immediately. I have toured all of the areas recently enough."

He leaned closely to her. He whispered so that no one else in the room could hear his words.

"No, my Queen. I believe that you have not been in this province in many years. The kingdom of the river people deserves the attention of the royal house."

When it dawned upon Lilith what he had done, she was speechless. How was it that this man read her every desire so quickly? She only had to think it and he somehow knew. A warm feeling engulfed her. She was so in love with him. Also whispering, she could hardly get the words out.

"What date does the Prince have planned for this important state visit? Is he sure that we can do this at this time?"

"Yes, I am very sure. It will be done quickly and quietly.

If we take swift horses and a party of no more than a dozen soldiers, we can be there and back before anyone in the capitol knows that you are gone."

She stood and took his hand. Raising it to her mouth, she kissed his fingers ceremoniously. The afternoon was not going to be devoted to state affairs. Arm in arm the royal couple walked to their private chambers. As usual, the servants and workers exchanged knowing looks. When the doors were closed, Lilith was like an exuberant child. She jumped up and down, hugging him.

"How did you know? Was it difficult to arrange?" her queries were filled with delighted laughter.

Samael's joy was reflected from his wife's boundless bliss. He had seldom seen her behave with such innocent exhilaration. The joy in her eyes when he gave her gifts had been nothing in comparison to this. Only the pleasure he saw in her eyes when she looked at him could match it. He thought that never in life would he see anything to compare with the beauty of her glee. His very life was now purposed to provide for her safety and happiness.

At times he tried in vain to remember any pleasant details of his life before her. There was nothing of note. If someone had told him that such emotion existed, he would have thought that person a fool at best. Had he been told that such a woman existed, he would have been sure of that person's addlebrained state. After their years together, she endeared herself to him in a greater way each day. Most importantly, he knew that his depth of feeling was reciprocated.

"You are agreeing to go on this journey, I presume?"

"Samael, you know me better than I know myself. Just as you arrived, my mind was drifting about. My thoughts have been on my kin for some time. I had accepted that travel was an impossibility. It has been so very long since I rested my eyes on my mother and father. Time has passed too rapidly.

I also want them to meet you. I need for them to know that I finally have love in my life. Even though I know that they have been long ago notified of our marriage, it is not the same. People marry for many reasons. It is important to me that they know that I love and am loved. They will know that my past history is no longer important."

Samael held his wife. They stood near a window in the warm glow of the sunlight. She was his very life.

At the darkest hour on a moonless night, the group quietly mounted the swiftest black steeds. Samael had chosen the dozen strongest, most loyal of his personal corps of soldiers. The entire party wore dark clothing to obscure any careless sightings. Lilith wore a dark hooded cape that disguised her well. Samael was careful to wear head covering to avoid anyone spotting the distinctive color of his hair. The most loyal of servants were sworn to secrecy. A ruse had been concocted to explain their absence. She had feigned illness publicly and was said to be confined to her bed for a period. Female absences were easily chalked up to the feminine biological mysteries. Since everyone in the kingdom was aware of their devotion, he was also explained as ensconced in her chambers with worry. The plan was to take the mountain route that was not well traveled. This would also enable Lilith to stop quickly and see her younger brother and his growing family.

Amazingly, the escape was made without discovery. Moonless nights alone instilled fear in many of the primitive people. Had they been seen, no one would have wanted to come close. Seeing a shrouded woman accompanied by thirteen men on black horses would have created a wave of terror on such a night. Samael executed his well-conceived plan perfectly. The route successfully kept them away from populated areas so that they were able to travel even during the day without detection.

When the fearsome group reached the grasslands that bordered to her childhood home. Lilith had the group pause to remove the dark and dreadful coverings. She did not wish to cause fear in her own people. They had traveled several days and arrived near dawn. Since they had stopped to change their attire, Lilith arrived looked every inch the regal creature that she was. The woman who walked up to her parent's home was even more beautiful than the daughter who had left so many years before.

Hana refused to believe her eyes. For so long she had wished to see her daughter just once more. Her health was failing and she was very aware that her time was limited. The gods had answered her prayers. When the headman looked into Lilith's eyes, his heart sang. The happiness and contentment that he saw reflected there gave him all answers that were necessary. He had hoped that his beloved child would someday find what she had not had with Adaama. He saw that it was so.

At no point in his long life had he been one to give weight to gossip, so he had ignored the wagging tongues eager to give information about his daughter's husband. Even though his old friend had told him good things regarding Samael, he truly believed when he saw it in her eyes. It was extremely difficult to believe that Lilith remained as lovely as she had ever been. Age seemed to have no effect upon her. He had to admit that she came of good stock. Hana had changed little in his eyes, but he was sure that love softened the picture. Nothing about Lilith's body had relaxed or enlarged in an unseemly manner. The line of her chin and neck remained firm and elegant. It was easily understood why she inspired such wild rumors throughout the land. He could not help but comment on the grand cape that she wore.

"I see that my daughter has sprouted wings. No wonder such rumors fly about the country. It is an amazing garment and explains a lot. After all these years, you appear beautiful and ageless, Lilith. Thank you for coming to see your old parents."

"Give the credit to my husband. Baba, this is Samael. He is the love of my life."

Samael blushed so that his face flushed to match the deep auburn shade of his hair. This was a new situation for him. She was the only family he had ever had. The headman was indeed the man of dignity of whom he had been told. His personal magnetism was enviable. The two men stood eye to eye. A look was passed. The headman touched his son in law's shoulder with warmth.

"I see that my daughter is in the best of hands. You have our belated blessings, my son."

Everything that he had read in his daughter's eyes, he saw reflected in her husband's. This big red haired man loved his daughter to no end. Samael's eyes filled with tears. Nothing had prepared him for the emotion of this moment.

It was important to him that he had inspired the trust of her father. He swallowed the considerable lump in his throat and put his arms around the older man.

"Sir, she is my very life. Before Lilith, I was a mere shell of a man. I promise that I will love and care for her unto death."

Lilith was overcome by the grave moment, but sought to lighten the mood.

"I appreciate that you both love me and I love you, but please stop before I break down. Mama, tell me about everybody." Removing her cape, she settled herself on a cushion in an un-queenly manner. She was home.

The headman took Samael from the dwelling. He led him and the soldiers to an area where the animals could be fed, watered and rested. After arranging for a feast to be set forth in the village common area, he stopped at the homes of various family members. When the two of them returned, her younger son and his little boy accompanied them.

Lilith could hardly believe that he had become such a man.

It was odd but he remained the same pleasant, laughing person that he had been as a baby. His pretty little wife

came behind them. She was again with child. The two of them

were equally dimpled and full of smiles. Lilith saw that they were genuinely happy. Her father spoke highly of the young man's abilities with the ivory knife, making his work among the most sought after in the village. He had begun to amass a very decent fund for his family's future.

Into the midst of the already crowded home came her brother's family. She was shocked to see her niece. Looking at the girl felt strange. It was as though she gazed into her own face. The girl was almost her mirror image. Only her huge brown eyes were different than Lilith's dark blue ones.

During the next day great feasting went on in the village. The Queen of the River was in her rightful place. Much was made of her handsome, devoted husband. Unattached local women enjoyed the company of Samael's soldiers since it was a rare occasion that so many visitors came to the village at one time. Lilith walked Samael through her steps of her early life. Her old dwelling had been lovingly kept in pristine condition, almost as a shrine to her. When she shared this space with Samael, all of the previous bad memories were swept away once and for all.

The royal entourage left by night as quickly as they had come. When Hana stood in the doorway watching the group of darkly clad riders, her heart bid goodbye to her daughter. At least this time she knew that Lilith was no longer alone. Her husband had ridden out part of the way with them. Her feeling was that he had some secrets to share with his favored child. Indeed, the headman spoke to Lilith of family affairs. She gave him her blessings to pass all other property to the sons and grandchildren. Also she left a ring to pass on to the one girl. Seeing her niece had struck a chord. She was consumed with a longing for the daughter that she never had. Once briefly, the feeling had come to her. Later, she had been relieved that it had not been so with Adaama. Suddenly she hoped that she was not past child bearing. She would like to have Samael's child. Naiimi had managed it. Just maybe it could happen for her. Then she remembered that she was queen. Her life was no longer her own. Her father turned back to the village, their goodbyes had been said.

The group arrived at her brother's village in the mountains by midday. Swift horses made a grave difference traveling. The journey was cut by more than half the normal time. Lilith had to insist that he curtail the degree of celebration he wished to indulge in. She greeted his people and had a short visit with his family. Leaving the mountain village, she reflected that her brothers seemed to have good lives. It was still strange to see that so much time had passed. Both she and the older of her two brothers actually had grandchildren now. She laughed when she realized that just a short time before, she had been considering having another child of her own. It was interesting to note that being in love tended to modify one's thought processes in many ways. It made her forget that she was now almost an old woman, a grandmother. As that thought circled around in her mind, Samael was looking lovingly at his wife. She was beautiful and desirable even under these circumstances. When they returned home to the palace, he would remind her once more.

The seasons blurred into one another. Years had folded into themselves. On this fall day a squat, muscular man came galloping up on a reddish colored horse. When the lone rider was admitted to the palace. He asked to see the queen, or her husband, immediately. When he insisted upon conveying his message personally, he was informed that the royal couple had gone to an outlying area. The day's task was to view the army that Samael had completely reorganized. He was determined that they be properly prepared to defend themselves against any strife that might arise.

When they returned to the palace. The queen was informed of the lone rider who had come to deliver some private message for the ears of either of the royal couple. When the muscular man was shown into her presence, Lilith's stomach dropped. The man was of her people, a man trusted by her father. One look at his face told her. Hana had died a few days ago. Her father had passed in his sleep that same evening. They died as they had lived, together.

26

L ILITH WAS UNCHARACTERISTICALLY subdued. Deep inside, she had somehow known that she would not see her parents alive again. Samael was the rock upon which she relied until she could adjust to her loss. When the mourning period was over, she plunged wholeheartedly into the day-to-day affairs of running her kingdom. Anyone who had known her would recognize her behavior as the same style that she had used when helping her father attend to the needs of the people of the river. No concern became too small for her attention. She moved among the people freely. Her popularity increased tenfold among the majority of her constituents. The people were a joyous lot. Anything that she could do to better the lives of the people was done. Her name was on every lip in the kingdom, becoming synonymous with all things good. One only had to hear *She,* spoken in a certain tone to know that the speaker referred to the Queen. Samael began to lessen his emotional degree of concern for her safety. She was no longer thought of as the Foreign Queen. Only a vocal few chose to resist her charms, making her truly popular for the first time during her reign. Pleasure was the watchword in the kingdom, as it was at the palace. The Queen ruled under the ways she knew best. Nowhere was she more loved than within the royal household. Those servants who worked directly for her were quick to let anyone know that the Queen was the best of all possible mistresses. They even gossiped less about the royal couple as time passed. It was apparent to all around them that their love was genuine. They were equal halves of a whole.

But the seeds of erosion had already been sewn. Most people in Saba had continued to worship the old gods. But throughout the surrounding lands, a new religion was springing forth and it began to catch on here and there in Lilith's own kingdom. Like a wildfire, it leapt through the people's hearts. The pantheon of ancient gods began to lose their luster. One god, Jehovah, became enough to satisfy the spiritual need of many of her people, too. Whispers were rampant among the servants. One after another, rumors began to point to various members of the royal household staff. A serving maid was found in a small room, praying to the god of the Judeans. The tearful girl was dragged before her Queen by the chief manservant, a Nubian named Bal. Interrupting the daily reports from the Treasurer, he burst into the throne room.

"My Queen, I must have your audience."

His voice boomed out in the relative calm, startling the poor Treasurer, who jumped and dropped his scrolls and boxes. Lilith, annoyed by the interruption to her routine, glanced across the room. Bal stood at the entrance to the room, his imposing form seemed to fill the space. His anger leapt across the space as his fingers clenched the reddened arm of the petite serving girl. Lilith sensed that this was no routine administrative issue. The young woman was tearful, but un-afraid. Despite the fact that Bal almost dragged her, she was resigned to whatever fate awaited her.

Lilith dismissed the Treasurer and summoned Bal forth.

"Bal, come forward. I do, however, insist that you unhand the young woman."

Her household was not one where servants were beaten, or other-wise mistreated. When he released the girl's arm from his grasp, Lilith beckoned to her. This situation disturbed her already. The girl, Shela, was known to her. She was a hard worker who was one of a legion like her attending to the needs of the household. Bal, though an organized and efficient administrator, on the other hand was sometimes imperi-ous. People like him were necessary to run a household as complex as that of the palace. Even though he had worked his way up to his cov-eted position of trust, Lilith recalled that his workers were sometimes heard to complain about him.

"Shela, what is the problem here?"

The young woman's face registered surprise and shock that the Queen addressed her directly. Bal became even more upset than he had been when he arrived.

"My Queen, I have no problem."

The girl stood quietly, massaging the reddened and bruised arm. Her composure gave Lilith pause.

She now turned to Bal, who stood fuming.

"What then, is your problem with this young woman, Bal?"

Wrinkles furrowed the forehead of the darkly handsome face that was just beginning to hint at aging. He had worked hard to attain the position of authority in the Queen's household. For years before this foreign woman's reign, he had labored in the household of the prior ruler. She dared to question how he treated a mere servant. He did not deserve such shabby treatment. It took every iota of dignity that he could muster to avoid making a dire mistake in addressing her.

"My Queen, this woman was caught worshipping the Judean god."

Lilith's face immediately registered a look of surprise. She regained her regal composure momentarily and thought about the situation. There were no laws prohibiting worship of this god, at least, not yet. These people were a source of irritation to her kingdom. Their priests believed in attempting the conversion of all about them. The concepts of asceticism and personal restraint were a large part of this growing monotheistic movement, neither of which was recognized by the majority of this pleasure loving society. A number of these priests sought to spread the word with the sword as often as with the tongue. More and more they were a source of acute concern. These warrior priests of the land of Judeah became more strident in their criticism against the queen they considered brazen. Their religious beliefs made Lilith particularly abhorrent to them. At this very moment, Samael was out in the countryside defending the kingdom against their incursions. Now the problem was literally in her own home. She looked at the girl before her.

"What do you have to say for yourself, Shela?"

The young woman's eyes widened in astonishment. Why was the Queen continuing to ask questions of her? What did she expect her to say?

"I can only say that it is true."

Her gaze was clear and proud as she looked up to the throne. Lilith had inherited the ornate chair made of gold. It had long been the seat of the nation's rulers, but this queen brought a specific elegance to it. Lilith's beauty was as imposing as the chair, yet this servant girl stood facing her without fear of rancor. Was it her belief that gave her such courage? Lilith thought for a few moments about the dilemma that she faced. Finally, she addressed the servant.

"Your appointment to service here has a specific set of tasks associated with it. You are not a slave. However, you are not paid to worship any god while you are here in the palace. Restrict your activities here to performance of your assigned tasks. Go on your way."

A collective gasp could be heard in the room. These people were undermining the way of life in Saba. Bal sputtered in protest.

"My Queen, but…but. She must be punished."

"Bal, I do not care about her beliefs. These people are a nuisance only in their persistent efforts to change all others about them. What would you have me do, kill her?"

The Nubian could not believe that Lilith could be so casual in her concern. These people sought to destroy the way of life supporting her reign. Her husband, the Prince, would not have been so lax.

"At the least, she should have been whipped."

Lilith stood to her full height. The fury contorting her lovely face was a terrible thing to see. Her indigo colored eyes clouded as dark as the sky of a summer storm.

"Never let me hear you refer to whipping any person in this household again! You do not have that authority! This poor servant girl and her one paltry god will not cause me to revert to savagery! Leave my presence now!"

Lilith, standing in her full and terrible glory, thrust her arm toward the door.

For an uncertain moment, Bal thought that she would jump down from the dais and physically attack him. The sheer fury of this woman was not something he had previously witnessed. He knew that she stood as tall as he did, but her strength was not something he had considered. At this moment he actually felt threatened by this deceptively beautiful foreign woman. Rumors circulated that she held her own wielding a staff and sword with her bodyguards. Her elite corps of guards was a well-trained group, each hand chosen by the Prince himself. Samael often engaged in combat exercises with them in the courtyard attached to the private barracks. Her highness had been observed in simulations of combat alongside him. It was said that she fought as well as any man. When he had heard the gossip, Bal had dismissed the bearers. He scoffed at the idea of a woman as beautiful as the Queen fighting with the troops. Today, he had glimpsed that face. He would never under estimate the foreign woman again. Turning quietly, the Nubian left the room quickly.

Lilith stood with her fists curled on her hips. Sunlight streamed through the highly placed window causing the circlets of gold on her wrists and head to cast gleaming reflections. Her posture was that of an enraged deity. The densely braided fall of hair masked one side of her face when she looked down at the space of floor vacated by Bal's exit. Those few left in the room saw that the intensity of her stare had not dimmed. In her mind she knew that the over reaction of such as Bal was further exacerbating the Judeans. Because her people did not understand the worship of this one god, they lashed out at the worshippers. There had been reports of persecutions all about the countryside. She did not know what was worse, the Judeans themselves, or the panic they caused. Lilith did not believe that the Judean priests should worry about what gods her people worshipped. Neither did she approve of her people persecuting their worshippers. If the priests would leave her country be, she would be happy. Her husband could find other ways to occupy his time. Lilith's preference was that she be his primary concern. She suddenly realized that regardless to the form it took, Samael's concern was for her. These priests truly despised her and they were a threat to her rule. Samael had been gone for over ten days protecting the border that joined Edom, now controlled by Judeah. His absence from her bed was a point of contention for Lilith. Today was ruined for her. Thanking her own gods that it was close enough to over, she summoned the masseuse. She retreated to her chambers in order to have at least some comfort given to her body.

After the masseuse left her quarters, she stretched out on her sleeping couch. By now the noises of the palace had quieted. In her head, Lilith reviewed the events of her day. The Treasury was in strong shape. Past reigns had focused more on ostentatious display. Lilith and Samael had made sure that the people were fed and that the government served its responsibility to its subjects. Though this country was gargantuan in comparison to the River Kingdom, Lilith utilized the principles that she had learned at her father's knee. Samael respected and supported her attitudes and opinions. He had begun to utilize more of the Treasury's funds to shore up the armies in order to protect the borders. Lilith's thoughts now turned to her own defense. The queen's personal guard was composed of a group of mercenary soldiers, who were funded from the royal couple's personal fortunes. Drawing from his past military experience, her husband knew that loyalties could become fractured between leaders and countries. He wished Lilith's guard to be loyal solely to her safety and their own. The dozen men that he eventually chose were the best of over one hundred who had applied for the choice appointments. Equal care and expense was invested in acquiring the tools necessary for this cadre of fighters who could function at the desired expert warrior level. Samael hired a man with whom he had served several mercenary campaigns in his youth. This seasoned warrior's sole function was to assist the Prince in outfitting and training these dozen warriors. Over a year's time he journeyed over the known world to acquire the best matched steeds. The fourteen strong black mounts that he ended up with, were the best money and breeding could acquire. It was their swift strength that had allowed Lilith the luxury of the surreptitious visit to her homeland before the death of her parents. Nowhere did a comparable match of a group of horses exist. Samael wanted to possess the ability to move quickly if necessary. The horses made this possible. Lilith worked with her husband to acquaint herself with the handling of the steeds. Unlike most of the men, she had limited exposure to the handling of the animals. Always during her first marriage, Adaama had taken responsibility for the animals. Samael knew that she needed a level of self-sufficiency for the current purposes. Lilith learned the practical side of caring for the animals quickly and a fast relationship was formed with her particular mount. Her husband found it remarkable that she took to every task with the same aplomb. She now cared for her mount as capably as she had sat in the saddle all along.

Lying in her chambers, Lilith continued to be restless and irritated. After the evening meal, she considered finding someone to take a ride with her, but Samael did not like her to be about the countryside without both himself and her personal guards. Even though she felt that he was excessively cautious, she understood that he was concerned because he loved her. Today's events would not lower his degree of concern any less. When she fell asleep, the thoughts of the servant girl were her last conscious ones.

She slipped easily into dreams. Lilith saw her childhood self, running merrily along with a group of other girls and boys. Peals of laughter created a delightful melody that rang across the village on a perfect morning in early spring. The sun had not reached its sometimes unbearable midday zenith. Everywhere brightly colored birds of many species flitted about the trees. Their multiple songs embroidered another dimension onto the loveliness of the day. Overhead fluffy clouds scattered about an evenly azure canopy of sky. Throughout the village a troupe of children ran and danced in circles. In the background the soothing, ever present sounds of the river could be heard. Lilith saw that she was the leader of this group, as she had always been in childhood. But now there were no adults anywhere, only the children at play. Because no one came to call them, the children began to fall as the sun became hotter and hotter. Finally only she was left standing. Even seeing her companions drop one by one, did not deter her. Face turned up to drink in the blinding light, she twirled faster and faster in her solitary dance. The sun seemed to descend to her level.

She felt herself come closer and closer. As the light engulfed her, she realized that there was no scorching heat, only an eerie incandescence. Suddenly, Lilith realized that she stood in the light totally alone. Her entire world was eclipsed. Not the birds, nor the trees, nor the village, not even the river had survived. Her dance stilled. She, too, fell.

Bolting upright out of the disturbing specter of her nightmare, Lilith ran from her bed. A throbbing pain seared through her temples. Grasping the large bowl used for night wastes, she leaned forward and emptied her stomach in wave after wave of wracking pain until only the odious green bile remained. Nausea continued to plague her, even after repeatedly rinsing her mouth with the sweet wine. At last, it passed. As she drifted down into the soothing vortex of slumber, for some reason her last conscious thought was the face of the girl, Shela.

Morning sounds of the palace stirring itself began to seep into the royal bedchamber. Lilith tentatively stretched her body in a feline manner, without opening her eyes. The night had been long and difficult. Dawn had barely begun to peek into the rim of the eastern sky. Just as she began to remember the disturbing dream, something else tugged at the edges of her consciousness. As her eyes popped open, her field of vision was filled. Sitting beside her, smiling and simply staring at her face, was Samael. His beard was scruffy streaks of rust with almost as much white mingled in. His handsome face was striped with the dust of the road. First she began to laugh aloud, and then cry. They held onto one another desperately. She covered his face in kisses, ran her fingers through his rusty curls. At no time could she remember being happier to see him. The words came rushing out in a torrent of gratitude.

"How long have you been here? Why didn't you waken me? You have been too long away from me."

The smile on his face reflected his total joy. He had pushed his troops unmercifully to cover the miles in record time. The ten days away had been painful. Whenever he could simply drink in the presence of her, he was happy. His thoughts had been amusing even to him. If anyone could have told him that his life would have taken such a turn, it would have been almost impossible to believe. He had just sat and looked at her for at least an hour. Because she slept so deeply, he didn't want to disturb his wife. His first inclination was to have someone prepare his bath and soak away the aches and pains of the ride. Time had interesting ways of injecting its presence. He had spent years on the road from one battle to the next. Walking, running, riding had made no difference. Still he held his own in any combat, but the body now felt different than before. His exhaustion had flown from his mind the minute he saw her.

Samael wondered if other men felt the same way about their mates. Could they possibly? He looked at Lilith in her perfectly exquisite beauty and knew that his wife was the most desirable woman who lived.

"I do not like being away from your side ever. As soon as I remove the dirt of travel, I promise to make it up to you."

Lilith drew his face to hers again. If he thought he could remain out of her bed even that much longer, he was a fool.

She proceeded to begin undressing him.

"No, you are mine, dirt and all."

Samael needed no other encouragement. The sweet streaks of the dawn became even sweeter. He was where he belonged.

When the royal couple opened their eyes to the rest of the day, the baths were drawn then the morning meal was summoned. Lingering over fruits and sweet seed cakes, they discussed the events of the past few days. Lilith decided that she would conduct no official business that day. Her husband was her entire agenda and that was that. She sent instructions to her staff. It had been awhile since she had been totally self-absorbed. She might lie in bed all day. These days, she amazed herself.

Samael had changed her life in every way. When she thought of the simplicity of her first life as Adaama's wife in the small dwelling in the village, it felt like someone else's history, not hers. She had been so starved for the passion that she shared with Samael. No, that could hardly be true since she had no idea that such a thing existed. Adaama's differences had consumed him, robbed him of joy. She truly hoped that he had conquered his personal demons and found some lasting measure of passion with his mirror image, Eve. Lilith laughed to herself when she realized how generous her spirit had become. The truth revealed to her mature self, was that every living creature deserved to be loved. It was much easier to feel that way from the perspective of her current life. Thank the gods for Samael!

Hardly a day passed that she did not thank every god in the roster worshipped by her people. This fleeting reflection of her own spiritual roots triggered another thought about the events of yesterday. Again, she questioned what could be so enthralling about this religion that was swiftly spreading about the world. Just as her husband re-entered the room, she realized that she had failed to discuss the incident with him. Samael listened quietly to her accounting of Bal's actions. After she described her own agitated response to the cruelty of the Nubian, he studied her momentarily before his reply.

"It does not surprise me that you defended the girl. But Lilith, I hope that you now understand how insidiously pervasive this Judean religion is. The girl could have been a danger to your safety. Some of these people are fanatics. It disturbs me that one of them is here in the palace. I believe that she should be replaced."

"Samael, she is just a girl who means no harm to anyone. She has served us well for two years now. Her work is no problem. She bothers no one."

"I understand your good heart, my love. But we must draw the line."

"She is no sword wielding warrior priest, but a young woman who supports her widowed mother and younger sister. Her life is not one of ease."

"The difficult straits of her life might be the very reason why this religion appeals to her. Lilith, those who live in such conditions are attracted by the principles of deferred reward. I will respect your concern for her, but I will not have her here. It is a danger to your safety. We will give her enough money to ease her situation."

"What are you saying, Samael? Is it that we buy the girl off?"

"Yes, as a matter of speaking, I suppose that I am. Your safety is my only concern. I will speak to Bal. We will give her a more than fair amount. If she is as devoted to her god as she says, it will be a relief for her to be away from us. Maybe her family can migrate across the border into Judeah. Then there will be fewer of them for us to worry about."

Lilith's face betrayed the ambivalent nature of her feelings. She knew that her husband was a good man and she must trust him.

"You are better informed than I am. Go ahead and do this, but I prefer that someone else handle it. Bal has already made himself the girl's adversary. If I were her, I would not trust him."

"Then it is agreed. My own man will handle this."

Samael went to instruct his personal manservant in the handling of the servant girl, Shela. Lilith watched as he strode from the chamber. She reveled in the distinct pleasure of his physical beauty. Age had not lessened the broad depth of his muscular chest and the bulging sinews of his strong arms. The mere sight of his body never failed to arouse her. Even now, satiated from the early morning's lovemaking, she felt the circles of desire began to clinch within her body. He would return soon to assuage them.

27

ALONG THE NORTHERN periphery of the kingdom lay the kingdom of Edom, which was continually at war with Judeah. The Judean forces were often as at home there, as in their own country. Troops remained busy in constant skirmish. The multitude of the manpower available to the priests never failed to amaze Samael. Today, his generals had come to the palace to review the plans for continued defense. It had become more and more difficult to maintain consistently high levels in that one location. Troops were needed to control the insurrections that had begun to erupt in the cities over the past two years. The constant friction between the factions of citizens was based upon which religion was practiced. Followers who worshipped the old gods would, from time to time, attack the worshippers of the one god. Mob mentality began to pervade the kingdom on all levels.

The divisive atmosphere had made Samael's job even more difficult. One entire troop of soldiers had to remain on assignment in the capitol. In order to placate the men, a rotation was established. Duty in the cities was more far desirable than camping along the barren, rocky borders. At this point, even the generals cast lots to trade the duty assignments. Samael called his leaders together to institute a reward system to encourage his army. Extended length of service at the front was cause for the award of funds of various sizes depending upon rank. The meeting commenced to the usual patterns. After a review of the various placements, Samael made some necessary shifts of leadership, then personnel. Contingency plans were put in place to protect each major city. The level of regard in which his generals held him, was apparent in the smooth transition of the meeting. The armies had stood firm against the increasing attacks of the Judeans.

At the conclusion of the meeting, he remained in the hall alone. So much swirled in his mind. Samael failed to understand what continued to fire the zeal of the priests. Thousands upon thousands hurled themselves against the northern borders. He had begun to supplement the kingdom's war chests with his own personal fortune. Lilith was yet unaware of the degree of involvement of the mercenaries. The country had begun to feel the effects of the campaign financially and emotionally. Citizens were on perpetual watch for the incursions of the Judeans. The wagging tongues of gossip accused one, then the other, of belonging to the foreign religion. Families were sometimes divided into fractious splinter groups. Samael questioned whether the kingdom would survive its self-inflicted attacks, deciding that these demoralized him most of all. At the back of his consciousness he began to harbor the possibility of removing his wife from the midst of this pandemonium. Beyond his duties of state, she was his wife before she was Queen.

In many ways he felt responsible for her presence here. He remembered the first time that he had seen her stride gracefully into the hall in that eastern city. From across the room he had experienced a sense of instantaneous recognition. In one moment he fleetingly glimpsed into the strangely colored blue eyes. It was as though, he saw her very soul and he knew her even then. Her beauty had haunted him from that day forward. She had been the toast of the evening's feast. Every other man in the room sought her attention while he had remained in the shadows and drank in her loveliness from some distance. His sources told him all that was known about the youthful Queen of the River. Who she was and where she came from, were facts of less consequence than the depth of intelligence he sensed accompanying her dazzling beauty. His evening's observance had brought him great pleasure, as even then Samael saw her grace and dignity. The special bond between she and her father was apparent from that distance and had fascinated him.

He thought back to the years he had spent alone. The memory of that young woman had fueled many of his dreams from that point forward, so he could barely believe his eyes when she re-appeared in his life. Even more unbelievable had been the development of their relationship over the months spent in the home of their friend. Initially, he had been afraid to hope for more than friendship. As he came to know Lilith, he sensed some reciprocation of feelings. Even then he was unsure. Because of the injuries, he remained hesitant. When he was absolutely sure that he loved her, he was willing to settle for any connection that would allow him to be in her presence. Sitting here in the present, even with the history that they had together, it was difficult for him to believe the amazing life that he had found with her. She was the woman of his dreams. Her beauty, sensuality, intelligence, sensitivity and bravery made her more than most men ever found in a life companion. By some strange twist of fate the gods had seen fit to give her to him. Eternally grateful, he wondered if she was his reward from the gods for his early suffering, but he also understood that it was his responsibility to care for her every need.

He rose from his seat in the now deserted room. Windowless and near the center of the palace, it was primarily used for secret staff meetings. He blew out the torches lighting the interior as he left. Walking along the corridor toward the royal chamber, he knew that what was necessary now was to assure the Queen's continued safety. But just for today, he could spend much needed time with Lilith. For the next few hours she would be only his wife. He would simply worship his beloved in every way that he knew.

As he neared the royal bedchamber, he found that his step had both lightened and quickened. When he entered, he found his wife sitting on the sleeping couch, legs crossed. In her hands was one of the large smooth silver trays that she used for looking at herself. The activity amused Samael to no end. She examined her reflection carefully and critically. Never before had he seen anyone do such a thing. She was her own worst critic. Despite the obvious attention that she had always received, she was not one of those women who centered upon themselves. A primary reason that he had fallen so madly in love with her had been her lack of self-consciousness about her beauty. He felt that she continued to see her rejected self when she looked at her reflection. Someplace deep inside her lived that young wife whose husband had not been capable of giving her the affection that she richly deserved. He knew what her first words would be right now. She looked up to see him enter with a quizzical expression on her face.

"Do you think that I am getting very old? Do I *look* very old, Samael?"

"No, darling. I don't. Besides if I thought that you were getting very old, then it would mean that I was absolutely ancient. If that were the case, we should simply find a quiet cave and die."

The rich baritone of his throaty chuckle filled the room. Just as he had thought, she was indeed seeing her inadequacies, not her beauty. His one regret was that they had not been able to share the experience of having a child together. Their friends had done so to their great joy.

Naiimi, Jahai and their son had visited them last year for a season. The reunion of Lilith and her best friend had been an exhilarating time. Even then as he saw his friend's deeply intense joy, he had been just one bit envious. Fatherhood would have been a remarkable experience and they would have created magnificent offspring. He would have liked to have a son with his red hair and her blue eyes. Their son would have been very tall and strong, a son to be proud of. Or a daughter, certainly one who inherited her mother's regal beauty would have been a source of phenomenal joy. Quickly, he brushed the tears that had formed in his eyes and begun to slide down his face. Just as promptly, Lilith jumped from the bed and rushed to him. He had not been quite as smoothly surreptitious as he thought. Her face was contorted in distress.

"What is wrong? What has happened?"

"Nothing really. You take me from laughter to tears in seconds. It is as though I did not live before you. I am sorry, it was just a nostalgic thought."

"What? What thought could cause you such pain?"

"No, it wasn't really *pain*, but maybe it was." He enclosed her in his arms. Looking straight into her eyes, he kissed the tip of her nose. "I thought for just one moment about what our possible children might have looked like. It was a bit overwhelming."

"Samael, I would have given anything to have been able to bear our child. It always seemed to me that I was so blessed by the gods to just have found you. Perhaps, in the next life."

The pair stood entwined in that same spot for a long while. Eventually, Lilith and Samael moved to the sleeping couch, where they lay in the same embrace until the last streaks of the day disappeared from the western skies. Today, the contentment of their shared presence was enough.

When the morning came, life resumed its old normal pace. The royal couple attended the ordinary business of the kingdom together. Samael's presence was reassuring to his wife as the administrative minutiae was handled. Time pushed days to turn into weeks, then months. The border skirmishes seemed to lessen, or the kingdom's troops were doing a more effective job of containing the intrusions from their war-like northern interlopers. Samael felt that his reward and rotation program was working effectively. He was satisfied to be able to remain in his own bed.

Meanwhile he began to investigate some alternative locations to live, just in case the activity increased. There were neutral cities where they could live far away. His political ties remained strong in most of the adjoining areas. He was ready to resume the life of a private citizen. Most of his adult life had been spent as a kingmaker. He had been first a soldier, then military advisor and warrior for hire. His merchant fortune came from those days. Since he had traveled the entire known world, his options were diverse. He did not want to worry his wife, but he knew that a contingency plan was the best idea. The larger cities near the west coast of the Red Sea seemed to be favored. They could blend in freely and anonymously. Here they could live in peace with people from many other cultures in a perfect climate. Living near the water always appealed to Lilith since she had spent the whole of her life in the same type of environment. It was time for the both of them to relax and enjoy the rest of their lives. After discussing the options with his wife, he began making plans. Lilith was delighted with the possibility of living near the water again. The remaining issue was the leadership of the kingdom. Samael felt that it was safest to have all plans solidified before letting go of the royal reigns. Just as he had brought Lilith forward all those years ago, he now quietly sought someone else to take her place. Only his very closest confidante was assisting him in this search. It would be a danger to them should any internal opposing factions know that such plans were afoot.

Along the northern border the quiet was merely a façade. Among the rocky outcroppings, the crafty Judean scouts sneaked past the now lax forces of Saba. They reported the state of Lilith's armies back to the Warrior Priests. Despite the rotation, a false sense of security was created by the lack of any direct confrontation in battle. The Queen's troops began to slack off their degree of vigil as the months passed. Around the nighttime campfires, the men of Saba allowed themselves to think of home. A spirit of merriment would take over as the skins of wine were shared. Music and laughter dulled the attention span. Camp followers had moved completely into the inner circle of the tents. At times it seemed as though the encampment housed a feast. Noises from the nocturnal activities totally masked the Judean troop movement when it came. The legions were crafty in their rapid, violent over run of the outlying camps. Once the first line of defense shattered, the advance toward the capitol was swift.

A loud clattering sound aroused Lilith and Samael up out of the deepest sleep. Realizing that there were two sources of noise. A thunderstorm raged outside. Usually, such storms were limited to the mountains. As unseemly as this occurrence was, additional noise was being caused by someone beating on the chamber doors. Samael leapt up and robed himself. First grabbing a handy weapon, he advanced cautiously toward the door. Lilith quickly pulled on a robe suitable for greeting. Her husband was now standing next to the door. He called out.

"Who is making such noise? Why do you beat at the door of the royal bedchamber? What do you want?"

"Prince Samael, I bring terrible news!" A distressed male voice cried out.

"Who are you? Of what do you speak?"

"I come from the camp of your general, Hamadi."

Hamadi was the general in charge of the northern territory. He was an old and trusted friend of Samael's. But many people knew that and might try to use the information to advantage.

"If you come from that camp, tell me when was your last rotation into the capitol?"

"We came on the first day of the summer festival. You met us at the edge of the city. Sir, you rode a different horse than the large black one that you rode upon your visit to our camp."

The poor man was absolutely accurate and sounded tearful at this point. Samael unlocked the door. Upon opening it, he saw a wet and bedraggled, but familiar face. Blood spatters and streaks covered his wet, grimy robe. Across his left thigh was a ragged, diagonal wound. He limped when Samael invited him in. Several of the palace servants stood anxiously in the background. The words came pouring out in a torrent as he whispered to Samael.

"The general is dead. Our camp was overrun and most were killed. I escaped only because I was the designated messenger. I know the quickest routes from the front and I have a fast horse. There are many, many of them, but most are on foot. They are, at the most, half a day behind me."

Samael did not pause. He asked the servants to care for the Messenger and explained to the assembled group that they should get away from the palace as promptly as possible.

He sent one of the men to summon the guard captain and went back to his wife. Lilith sat on the edge of the couch. Her large eyes were widened even further. She had heard some of the man's words. She realized what was next and sat to compose herself for just a mo-ment. As he approached her, she spoke up.

"It has happened, I gather."

"Yes, we must go. I am sorry that it came to this."

"We need only to dress. Everything has been prepared as we dis-cussed. The packs only need to be loaded onto the horses. I will be dressed in the blink of an eye."

At that moment, three of the men who served as the Queen's Guard came in. The captain stationed the two men at the door. "Sir, the horses are being readied. When you and the Queen are

ready, we await you in the courtyard. These two will accompany you."

Lilith had adjourned to the other room and emerged in her dark colored traveling skins and cape, ready to make the escape as planned. Samael disappeared to don his similar set of clothing. They were clad in the darker colors in order to be the least visible at night. She looked about the room. The only jewel that she bothered to take was the large red stone Samael gave her at the beginning of their love affair. The state jewels belonged to the kingdom and were not her concern. She also packed the remainder of the precious ivory pieces that her father had hoarded for her. Included in them was the creamy aged comb that had been passed down in her family. Because they had known that this day would come, their personal funds had been sent ahead to be held for them. Merchant friends in two different locations were prepared to assist the royal couple in their resettlement. All personal plans were in place. It was simply necessary to arrive in either of the proper locations. The party now made quick work of their departure. Goodbyes were said to the royal staff. Bequests were given for the years of loyal service. These people had become a surrogate family in many cases. Some of the partings were difficult, but finally they rode away. Thirteen men clad in black, accompanying one dark shrouded figure, rode on massive black horses into the stormy, misty night.

Lilith considered the panorama that her life had been. Now she was off to yet another segment of the adventure. It would be a good thing to settle in some non-descript house near the sea. She and her husband could grow old quietly, without the responsibility of governing a country. Perhaps she might even see more of the grandchildren that her youngest son had given her. There was also the myriad group of nieces and nephews, most of whom she barely knew. This chapter in her life would be wonderful.

As the assemblage of riders exited the capitol on the eastern road, chaos had begun. Even in the rain, fires were visible in the far northern villages bordering the capital city. In the zeal to free this country of the Foreign Queen, it was apparent that the Judean army was being very thorough. Samael expected them to become less bloodthirsty once they saw that the country was free of the ruler that they found so abhorrent. He was, in fact, counting on it. It was not his wish that the ordinary citizens suffer. It was paramount that the plan of escape work just as they had put it in place. Nothing could have helped them more than the sudden unusual storm. Now the lightning bolts crackling in the sky kept the population indoors. Few, if any, would see their escape. Any that did catch a glimpse of the fearsome entourage would be intimidated and avoid contact with them at all costs. Especially in the outlying areas, the people were simple in their beliefs and understanding. Along with the guard captain, he pushed this group to a furious pace as they rode. The route that was mapped out would take them first out of the city in the direction of the nearest city to the east, then to turn sharply to the southwest. If they could get undetected to the southern port city of Mocha, a boat had been arranged to go from there by sea. His hope was that this would satisfy the Judeans. An easterly flight was to divert anyone from the knowledge of the eventual destination. Once the group reached the midway point, they would part ways. The majority of the mercenaries would be free to go about their own way. Only the captain and three others would accompany Samael and Lilith to the south, where they would depart alone, in anonymity, to the city where they had chosen to live out their lives.

Pushing their mounts to the edge of exhaustion, the group rode through the night. Samael felt good about their progress. No one had accosted them on their path. Neither did he detect anyone following them. At dawn, they stopped in a dense stand of trees and made camp. They would eat, then rest for the bulk of the day. As long as they stayed away from the main road, all should be fine. As the day ended a scout would back track to ascertain that no one was on the trail behind. Once this was done, the group could move forward.

Lilith found a comfortable spot to rest. Her royal status had not softened her to the point that she had any difficulty finding ease in this situation. Each task was dealt with as it came. She was about to sink down into sleep, when her husband found her. He came and created a nesting spot for himself.

"Are you able to rest here?"

His voice was filled with care and concern. Even though he had known what the trip would be like, he wanted the best for her always. Lilith smiled dreamily, understanding and appreciating why he asked.

"Darling, I am fine and almost asleep. Do not be wary of my comfort. I am strong and healthy. Go to sleep."

With that she kissed his hand and drifted into slumber. For a few moments, her husband lay quietly next to her. Thankful that the plan was working so well, he too soon slept.

When Lilith came awake, Samael was already up and gathered with the men. As she came up, she saw that the scout had returned already. It was near dusk and it appeared that all was in readiness to resume the journey.

"Why didn't you awaken me? I have delayed the progress of the journey. My sleep was probably too deep to be healthy anyway."

Samael put his arms about her shoulders, kissing her cheek. The men noticed how openly affectionate the royal couple always were. Nothing seemed to cause a rift between them.

Among their guard, the general consensus was that the relationship was one to be envied on all counts. Most of the reason that they were loyal to the Queen had to do with their great admiration of her as the perfect woman. The captain turned to her and offered her assurance.

"My queen, Do not..."
She did allow him to finish, but looked directly at him in a sincerely honest fashion.

"I am no longer your Queen. My name is Lilith. Address me as such. You are now my friend and associate, not my subject. We are all embarked on a perilous course together. It is unnecessary to add artificial formality to the situation."

The men were aghast, but somehow not surprised. She had always been fair and decent to them.

"Madam, I will find it hard to take such liberty."

"Nonsense. If I grant you the privilege, it is not a liberty. What did you mean to tell me?"

"Only that the scout saw no sign of troops following us. We will proceed. The rainstorm would have wiped out any tracks anyway."

Lilith thought to herself that there was only the one major road in that direction. Tracking wouldn't really be necessary. She smiled graciously and went to mount her horse. Travel was tiring, but there was no choice. They once again started out, rested, fed and with freshened steeds.

Relentlessly, the pounding rhythm of the hooves continued east. It had begun to wear on the travelers. At least now the weather was normal. After the first night of fearsome storms, the skies had cleared to the normal clarity. Only the distance began to weigh upon their spirits. Finally, the city was in sight. The group split into two. Both Samael and the captain were satisfied that the escape had gone undetected. No sign had been seen of the Judean armies. They were smugly content that all was well. As suddenly as the appearance of the summer storm over the capitol had been, the circumstances turned. In the distance were soldiers, visible as far as the eye could see. Only the Judeans could amass such a gargantuan group. Perhaps the attack had been two pronged and this was the second wing of the army. It was possible that they had come along the coast on the frankincense route and then turned inland. There was always the possibility that they had been betrayed, and the invaders knew to look at Mocha. Samael knew that the right amount of gold bought almost any information, so he would not rule this out. As quickly as the invaders were spotted, they turned the mounts to go north. His horses could outrun the approaching throng, but the question of the location of the original assemblage remained. In a straight northerly direction, they would hit the deserts of Edom. If they could turn sharply at the last minute, the northern ports of the Red Sea would be accessible. It would not be the wise course, but it appeared to be the only one. Fleeing the first approaching soldiers they had headed due east, so it did not seem logical that they could return in that direction. Further east routes would be less safe. Besides the distance to the next settlement, it would be harder to reach a port city. The best chance for avoiding the Judeans would be to go north, then sharply west. If the few of them could shadow the road without actually accessing the thruway, it might be possible to survive. Samael was truly concerned that so much effort was being put forth to find them. That thousands of men were deployed to find just Lilith and him did not bode well. Travel was beginning to wear on them. Supplies would now dwindle quickly. According to the original plan, they should safely be aboard the vessel by now. Instead an unknown number of days of travel and unquestionable hardship lay ahead.

Knees pressed frantically into the glistening blackness of the horses' flanks, they rode north. Before this the air of the flight had been urgent, but now certain desperation seeped into the actions of the travelers. Across the countryside they rode. Bodies strained closer into the manes of the horses seemingly in an attempt to meld with the mounts. Above, the glare of the morning sun increased to a midday burn. The rays bore into their backs, causing the clothing to stick and bubble like fabric blisters to overheated flesh. Head coverings served the dual purpose of shading the eyes from glare and protecting the heads. Being pushed well past the normal rest periods, the horses breathing became audibly stressed. All were exhausted, yet no one dared admit the level. Finally, as the group approached a verdant area with a source of water, they paused to refresh themselves and the horses. There was no casual conversation. Only the facial expressions spoke to one another. The guard captain spotted the signs of a very recent campfire and came to tell Samael, who sat beside his wife. They had obviously been in quiet conversation.

"Sir, I believe that our men only recently left this place. We should catch up to them before dusk, if we do not take leisure for too long a period."

"That would make sense. However, I am not sure that we should attempt to involve any more people in our dilemma.

In fact, Lilith suggests that you and the men should leave us now. We, alone, are the quarry sought by the Judeans."

"Sir, each of us signed on to protect the Queen. None of us were Sabeans. She is still the same person. This was the job we signed on to do. We understood from the beginning what it entailed. We will not abandon her, or you."

At this impassioned speech, he bowed deeply to Lilith. She rose from her resting place and touched his shoulder.

"Please, I can't be responsible for your deaths. I ask that you all go ahead. You should be able to overtake the rest of the men."

The soldier looked up at her for a few seconds. His voice rang with clarity and pride.

"We will do no such thing. The men and I have already agreed upon our course of action. When you are rested we will proceed."

He turned and walked back to the others. After a short period, the entire group climbed aboard the horses. Roads going in this direction skirted the very edge of the desert. The trail sometimes narrowed to barely wide enough for two horses to ride abreast. To the far north of the road, the red deserts were visible. Samael wished to avoid this area because of the ugly sandstorms that could rise in seconds. Not only could travelers get completely lost, but the severe *samoons* could literally drown them in sand. The riders now crisscrossed to cut to the upper coast of the Red Sea. Some willing foreign captain would accept gold to transport the royal couple. The soldiers could blend into the population of the port cities without effort, as a mere change of clothing would render them indistinguishable from the myriad of others. Here at the ports, Nubian, Phoenicians, Sabeans, Egyptians blended with others from the various countries near and far.

In the distance a column of dust could be seen coming toward them. This could only mean that a large party was ahead. Realistically, it could only be another company of Judeans. Armies were ahead and behind them. Simultaneously, The riders cut from the main road north. As they did they spotted the others of their original group, headed in the same direction. The only chance was to use the speed of the mounts to outrun the foot soldiers. Just then, Samael spotted a large mounted contingency break out from the Judean troops to give them chase. Lilith could hear her heart pounding in tune to the rhythmic pounding of the horses' hooves. By now they had re-united with the others and all were riding forward with fierce resolve. She held her own with the men. The guard captain called out from the rear that the Judeans were gaining on them. It was possible that their mounts were more rested. Suddenly ahead of them loomed a rocky outcropping. There were numerous caves in this desert area. There was little hope that they could continue to out run the invaders. There were thirteen men and one woman against thousands. If they could conceal themselves in the caves until nightfall, perhaps there was some small possibility that they would survive. The group cut in and out of the rocks until they found the mouth of a likely cave. As dusk crept in, a decision was made. Closer behind them, the shouts of the soldiers could be heard. The group slipped into the cave while one of the men took the reins in an attempt to lead the group of soldiers away from the rest. Samael hoped that the cave might be the entry to a network of the catacombs that networked along the border of Edom. Descending into the depths as far as possible, no outlet was found. This cave was not their answer. Rocks had been rolled to cover the mouth. Quietly, they crouched in the darkness. They needed only escape detection. Maybe the Judeans would pass by them in the night and continue on their way. Hours passed. The group fell asleep in the semicircular format against the rear of the cave. No fires could be lit. Skittering bats, snakes and small rodents were heard throughout the night. Lilith awoke to find a large spider crawling on her arm. Without a second thought, she slapped it. Lying there she realized that no noise had been heard that would have signified thousands of men in the area. The young man who had taken the horses was going to create a false trail, then attempt to circle around to bring back the horses once they were lost. He claimed to know the hills well from having grown up in the area. Lilith prayed to her gods for his safety. Except for the faint symphony of the breathing of the men, it was quiet. Even the cave dwelling insects and animals seemed to settle down. By her reasoning it should be dawn soon. Glancing down beside her, she saw her husband lying with his head resting against her abdomen. The streaks of light should be visible around the rocks soon, she thought. Just then, Samael stirred and looked immediately up to her face.

"Good morning. How long have you been awake?"

His smile was a beautiful thing to behold. His teeth gleamed brightly in the dim light. She leaned forward and kissed his forehead.

"For a very short while. I have heard no activity. Do you think it is possible that we escaped them?"

"It would be a miracle. I have lived through tighter situations. One never knows. But as a reminder, I love you. Thank you for what our life together has been so far."

At that moment, Samael put his finger to his mouth. Some sort of a scratching sound came from the mouth of the cave.

The first streaks of light could be seen in the miniscule patch of sky visible around the edges of the rocks they had used to cover the opening. One by one, he touched the guard contingency awake. The smooth rock that made up the cave floor made it easy for the men to stealthily rise. Holding the weapons at ready, they approached the opening. Lilith did the same. Samael raised his sword. Just as he was about to lunge, a piece of gear belonging to the royal guard was rolled into the opening. A collective sigh of relief went up from the group.

"Sir?" a whispered voice said. It was the young soldier who had taken the horses ahead the night before.

"Come in quickly!"

Samael and the men rolled the largest of the rocks back quickly. He slipped in.

"I have the horses, sir."

"But where are the Judeans?"

The captain of the guard asked. He attempted to see around the small patch of light.

"Sir, I am not sure. They are not about. I did not see them again when I left with the horses."

"I don't like this. They were close upon us. At any moment I expected them to swarm into the cave. Could they possibly have missed the last turn that we made? Is it truly possible to get hopelessly lost in these rocks and hills?"

The captain shook his head. Samael nodded his head in agreement. It did not seem that they could have been so clever.

"Perhaps you and I should go out and survey the surrounding area."

"No, I will go. How far away are the horses?"

The young scout replied and started back toward the opening.

"Sir, they are only a few moments' hike. I will go with you. We can lead them back. The others can be ready to quickly hop astride."

The two men left the cave, first looking in all directions.

The group huddled near the opening, waiting for them to return. Shortly, the noise of the hooves was heard. As the group emerged from the shelter of the cave, men swarmed from the rocks above them and around them. The Judeans attacked them full force. Their patience served them well.

Employing every weapon available to them the thirteen men fought valiantly. When the warrior priests began their attack, Samael's men first stood firm. As the attack strengthened, his force began to fall one by one. Well trained though they were, these mercenary soldiers were no match for the soldiers of Judah, who fought with the zeal of belief. The warrior priest came with hordes of fervent followers. Samael fought valiantly. The skill of his many years' mercenary campaigns kept him alive. Despite his extraordinary effort, he could not withstand the sheer numerical advantage of the attackers. Backed into the mouth of the cave, he made a courageous stand to defend his wife. Three of the opposition attempted to overcome the strength and skill of Samael. Finally, a fourth approached him from the rear to deliver the ultimate blow. As the big man crumpled to the rocky red surface, his eyes turned to see his beloved for the last time. His mouth formed a guttural plea to the enemy.

"Please spare her," he said as he fell.

But Lilith was not a coward. Even as she saw his blood ooze out onto the rusty sand, she continued to fight. The first howl that came from the deepest reaches of her soul startled the warriors. The dark sound tore from her being to grieve the loss of her other half. Screaming vengefully, she grasped the sword and staff with all of her remaining strength. Like some mythical mad creature from nightmares she wielded her weapons artfully and vigorously. In her last moments she was the epitome of the Warrior Queen. Valiantly, she stood and fought beside her husband's body, to the death. Her last sight was the brilliant shards of the morning sun as they flashed over the red mountains. As the light filled her eyes and blotted out her vision, she remembered the last dream. She danced in the blinding light until she too, fell. The invading army overcame what remained of the small force, hacked them to pieces and scattered their carcasses to the winds. The idol worshipping Foreign Queen was dead. Lilith and Samael rested together in the deserts of Edom with the company of the jackals and vultures for eternity. The Wagging Tongues could finally rest. *She* was no more.

The End

EPILOGUE

H ER ADHERENCE TO the old ways, her worship of the pantheon of old gods sealed Lilith's fate. She and her consort epitomized the hedonistic, pleasure-centered life. In a time when life quickly took such exacting toll on the human body, she not only retained her splendid good looks, but also flaunted them. Her penchant for wearing of bright colors and jewelry offended them. In societies where woman was little more than chattel, she dared to walk among men. They chose to believe that she was at fault for Adam's desertion, though he had fled with the girl, Eve. Because she did not allow the tragedy of her abandonment to destroy her life, she was labeled an adulteress. She then dared to love a man who was considered irreparably damaged by society. Because he had found peace with no other woman, they believed that he was incapable and labeled Lilith as demon. Gossip and ignorance were the twin destructors of Lilith's regime. As the new religion took hold in Saba, the priests gained strength.

The version of this woman's story passed down through history was that of Adam's ancestors. As the translations were repeated through time and ancient languages, further distortions were probably made with each version. Until finally she was obliterated completely by name. It is said by some scholars that this one reference to Lilith remains in the King James Version of the Bible. It is a chronicle of the destruction of her kingdom by the warrior priest Jacob.

"… and all her princes shall be nothings… And thorns shall come up in her palaces, nettles and brambles in the fortresses thereof…the satyr shall cry to his fellow …the night monster shall find for herself a place of rest…" Isaiah 35:12-14.

ABOUT THE AUTHOR

A PRODUCT OF DUSTY South Texas, Darlene Dauphin has been telling "stories" since she was a small girl. Since she became a prolific reader early in life, she developed insatiable interests in history, poetry and the world at large. After retiring, newly repatriated to the Gulf Coast, her creative juices truly began to flow and she began her second act as a Performance Poet, speaker and Author. Her first novel, *Emilie's Song*, was published in 2008 and expects to soon release two other novels, as well as a volume of poetry.

38720046R00132

Made in the USA
Middletown, DE
12 March 2019